JANICE WHITEAKER

THE LOST BOYS SERIES

FINDING
What's Mine

Finding What's Mine, Book 1 of the Lost Boys series

First printing, 2019
Cover design by Robin Harper at Wicked by Design.
Editing by April Bennett at the Editing Soprano.

For all the lost boys trying to find a way to be good men.

1

Tracker

FUCK.

I watch from my post at the bar as the reason I'm here climbs up on a table in the corner and starts shaking her ass. Her skin-tight black jeans leave little to the imagination. Not that the sequined crop top barely covering her top half does much better.

She pauses to sip at the tiny straw stuck into the drink clutched in her hand and I take the opportunity to look around. See if anyone besides me is paying a little too much attention to daddy's angel. That's what I've decided to call

Kerosene Danger Wallace.

Her daddy sent me to make sure she stays safe while he cleans up a mess he made. A mess I should be helping figure out instead of sitting in a hole-in-the-wall bar in a college town trying to blend into a place I clearly don't belong. Never did. Never will.

I catch Kerri teetering on the edge of the table out of the corner of my eye. She's trying to step down but with a drink in one hand and her purse slung over the other it's a little more complicated of a move than she can handle four cocktails in.

That's how I know this girl isn't as wild and crazy as she wants to look. Four drinks over two hours isn't how you drown.

As she starts to teeter in her heels I slide off my seat. Before I can get any farther a chubby dude with thick glasses and a half-ass beard rushes in to save her, holding out both arms to catch daddy's angel as she goes down in a suspiciously practiced looking tumble.

Maybe someone was watching her after all.

I size the man up as he carefully helps Kerri get her footing. She blushes and drops her eyes to peek at him through the thick black mascara-coated length of her lashes. It's obvious she's in no rush to get out of his embrace. Her hero's ears turn red as Kerri wraps her tattoo-covered arms around his neck, leaning heavily against the man who saved her from the unfortunate fate of meeting a sticky, beer-soaked floor.

I sit back in my seat and polish off my beer, letting my eyes move around the room, scanning again for anyone that looks like they are planning to cause problems for me. All I see is college kids enjoying their Friday night out after a week of taking classes on mommy and daddy's dime at the prestigious institution less than a mile away.

"Fuck me." I shove my empty bottle to the back of the bar and stand up. I need to stretch my legs. Might even take a piss while I'm up. It's been a long fucking night watching kids living a life I could only dream of.

If I was stupid enough to dream.

The path to the bathroom takes me right past the table where daddy's angel and her hero are now all over each other.

That escalated quickly.

I listen carefully as I pass and have to stifle a grin. Hero's in over his head on this one. Kerri's voice is smooth and strong as she coos in his ear leaving the guy a stuttering mess.

Good for her. At least someone's having a nice evening.

I make my way through the heavy crowd of academics filling the bar well beyond what the sign on the wall says is maximum occupancy. It's nearly impossible to move without bumping into a college student in a hoodie chugging a microbrewery labeled beer. If anyone's here to grab my club president's daughter they're going to have a hell of a time even getting her out of the place before I intervene.

And I will.

That's my job now. To keep Kerri safe. No matter what it takes.

The bathroom hallway is surprisingly deserted. The noise from the crowd in the bar is a low thrum here making it seem quiet and secluded. I turn to give the doorway one last check before I reach the men's room door. I can barely see daddy's angel and hero still cozied up.

This job might not be as difficult as I expected it to be.

I barely get the men's room door open before I'm hit in the back by the full force of a body against mine, shoving me into the single toilet bathroom and against a window on the opposite wall a few steps away. I barely spin in time to catch the mother fucker who just made the worst decision of his life.

But the body pressed into mine isn't there for a fight.

"Hey." The word passes through full cherry red lips. It's breathy and soft, like the sweet push of the breasts against my chest. "I think you're in the wrong place mister..." Chocolate eyes sweep over my face and down my neck dragging over the lines of the only tattoos visible with the crisp button down and jacket I wear.

My club tattoos.

"Tracker." I hold still as her hands press into my chest, warming my skin through the thin cotton of my shirt. I think I might sit back and let her run the show. She started it and I'm happy to ride in the passenger seat with this one.

Maybe happy is the wrong word.

I'm smart enough to know women like this look at me a certain way, expecting I can give them something their pretty-boy boyfriends can't.

And they're right.

I know my place in this world. It's between her legs, not in her life.

"Tracker." She smiles as she repeats my road name.

I love the sound of it as it rolls off her tongue. I can think of a few other things I would love to have rolling off her tongue.

"That's an interesting name." She moves her body over mine as her hands slide up my chest and along the lapels of my jacket. "Is it biblical?"

I'm confused for a second until I see the spark of humor in her brown eyes. I give her the sexy smirk I know women love. "Funny."

She presses against me with a surprising amount of force, the soft curve of her belly rubbing against my dick in a way that makes me groan and forget my decision to ride shotgun on this encounter. I reach around and fill my hands with her ample ass, squeezing the full cheeks as I grind my cock against her. I watch with satisfaction as her pupils dilate in the glow of the bathroom's fluorescent light.

Her skintight red dress rides up as I palm her bottom and look her dead in the eye. "What did you come here for?"

She leans into my chest, her tits pushing up high and full, threatening to break the levy of the low-cut neckline on her dress. "For you, Tracker."

And then she fucking puts those cherry red lips on mine, eating at my mouth like she skipped dinner. Her tongue rubs over mine. She tastes like vodka, RedBull, and bad decisions. I fucking love it.

As her mouth leaves mine she sucks my bottom lip between her teeth, holding it until it pops free. She licks her lips and I wonder what they'll look like wrapped around my dick tonight. She smiles slowly. "And what did you come here for, Tracker?"

Fuck.

I forgot about daddy's angel in the next room.

"Business."

Her brows go up. "Interesting place to conduct business."

"I'm an interesting man." I tease her a little. Run my hand up her ribcage letting my thumb graze over the side of her breast. She's just the kind of woman my dick gets hard for. Soft curves and full hips that can take anything I want to dish out.

"Maybe we can get to know each other a bit." She sucks in a breath as my thumb rakes across her nipple. Her bottom lip disappears between her teeth as I tease the tight nub through the flimsy fabric of her dress.

"I'd like that." I let her rub against me a second longer before I flip her around, switching spots, pressing her back against the large window. I pull up the hem of her dress without resistance. I want to show this woman what I can do for her. Give her a reason to leave with me tonight.

I need something good in my life right now and she's the best-looking thing I've seen in a while and for some reason she's here with me instead of one of the pretty boys filling the bar. I want to prove she made the right decision.

I look down at the thin strip of red lace covering her pussy. I drag one finger up the scrap of fabric, tracing the seam of her cunt before tucking it under the elastic waistband. When she doesn't try to stop me I slip my hand into those hot as fuck red lace panties I can't wait to rip off her.

She gasps as I slide my fingers along the hot folds of her pussy. She's soaking wet and I can't stop myself from pushing deep inside her.

Her head falls back against the window as I find her clit with my thumb and start to work it. The tiny bit of flesh swells and hardens under my touch as I continue to finger fuck her at the same time. She barely makes it thirty seconds before she's coming on my hand, grabbing my shoulders for support.

I suck on the bit of skin tucked behind the gold earring dangling from her lobe. "Can I buy you a drink?"

Her body twists side to side as she pushes her dress back in place. "You can." She pulls me in by the front of my shirt for one last heated kiss. "I'm going to the ladies to freshen up. I'll meet you in the bar."

I walk out of the bathroom after her. Red dress disappears into the next room over and the door lock clicks into place. I adjust the open collar of my button up shirt and straighten the lapels of the suit jacket I figured would do a little to soften my look. The smell of summer air drifts up from the place my hallway surprise pressed her body against mine. I breathe in the fresh scent of flowers and sunshine as I pass daddy's angel on my way back to the bar. She and her hero are still wrapped around each other, swapping spit like no one's watching.

As far as she knows no one is.

I tend to agree.

I slide back into my seat. The bar's finally starting to thin out as it nears closing time, making it easier to keep an eye on the men milling around.

And watch for a tight red dress that should be headed my way any second. Hopefully daddy's angel and her hero time their evening right and I can fuck red dress in my car outside Kerri's apartment, wherever that may be.

Two birds. One stone.

Tonight is one of the few times my lot in life works out in my favor. Women like red dress might not want to take me home but they're happy to let me fuck them any place else.

I check my watch. It's been ten minutes and red dress is still in the bathroom. I give her five more before I go check on her, shaking my head at hero as I pass by. Hopefully he enjoys tonight because it's a story he'll be telling for years. The night a hot girl sucked his face off in a bar.

As I walk into the bathroom hallway a woman walks out from the ladies room. A woman not wearing a red dress.

I point to the door. "Anyone else in there?"

She turns to look at the door then back at me. She shakes her head. "It's a single."

I walk past her in disbelief and shove the heavy wood door open wide. The room's identical to the men's. Same single toilet. Same single window, cracked open to let out the stale air of the crowded bar.

And no gorgeous woman in a red dress that smells like springtime.

It stings more than it should. Not because of the aching balls in my pants but because it's a harsh reminder of what I am.

And what I'm not.

Kerri and her hero are just scooting out of their seats when I walk back into the bar. My mood is souring by the second. And I was already sour when I got here. The tiny bit of a bright spot I had in the bathroom now makes everything worse in comparison. Darker.

Lonelier.

Daddy's angel leads hero through the crowd. He scurries after her like a puppy dog. I lag behind, giving the bar one last scan for a red dress before I slip out the door unnoticed.

She's gone. A few minutes alone in the bathroom was probably all it took for her to come to her senses. Remember she was the kind of woman who liked smart boys instead of bad men.

The night air is still warm as I walk outside to the barely lit parking lot beside the bar. I already know where Kerri's car is parked. It's how I knew she was here. As luck would have it I passed this bar on my way into town and what did I happen to see sitting in the lot? The very car my contact at the DMV said belongs to a Kerri D. Wallace.

Can't say I blame her for the name change. Hell, it would be easy to believe the entire reason Kerri hates her daddy is because he fucking named her Kerosene. But I know better. I know her daddy and I would say her list of reasons to hate King is as long and varied as my own.

I stop in my tracks and stare at the spot where Kerri's car was parked a few hours ago.

The black four-door sedan is gone.

I watch in disbelief as daddy's angel pushes the button on a fob and unlocks a high-end sporty two-door. She slides into the driver's seat and hero jumps into the passenger.

I spin in a circle searching for Kerri's car. It's gone. She's gone.

And I'm fucked.

Because it turns out daddy's little angel isn't who I thought she was.

2

Kerri

"MS. WALLACE?"

I turn around and find one of the older students in my class standing in the doorway to my office.

"Do you have a list of tutors who could help me wrap my head around this stuff?"

Crap. I knew there was something I forgot to do. I give him an apologetic smile. "I do but it's not been updated for this semester yet." I search around my desk for the last list our department compiled, shifting papers on my normally tidy workspace that has recently become a black hole of office supplies and empty diet soda cans. I keep talking as I rifle through papers hoping this man isn't quietly judging me for the wrecked state of my office. "I'm sure most of them are still willing as long as they're still here."

This mess is not like me. Not like the me I try to prove I am anyway. I need to get a grip and get everything back in its place. My work. My apartment.

My freaking sanity.

I see the bright pink flyer and snatch it from the bottom of the stack of crap it's hidden under. Thank God we printed it on the obnoxious color of paper. I'm going to have to remember to do that next time. Not that I plan on needing to find it in an avalanche of papers again.

I hold it up in the air. "Got it." I hand the roster to Carlos. "If you have problems finding someone let me know and I'll see if I can set something up."

He grins at me and takes the paper from my hand. "Thanks. This is a whole lot harder than I expected." He scans the list. "I bet most of these people are half my age."

"And probably bombing half their classes." I pat him on the shoulder as we walk out of my office together. Older students are my favorite. They work harder. They are more respectful. They are serious about being here. "All this work is going to be worth it." I smile at him. "I promise."

Carlos dips his head in a nod. "I know it will." He holds the paper up as he walks down the hall giving me a grin. "Thanks again, Ms. Wallace."

This is why I need to get my head together. People like him are counting on me to help them better their lives. Get a fresh start. Build a future.

It's something I understand more than they realize.

I turn back to the shambles my office is in. It's amazing how quickly it can all spiral out of control. How quickly *I* can spiral out of control. I hoped after all this time and practice I was different. Better.

That I fought genetics and won. It looks like I will have to keep fighting.

Maybe forever.

I blow out a breath as I slip off my pumps and wiggle my toes. I might as well stay and straighten up. Not like I have anything exciting waiting for me at home. I rub my eyes and try to remember that it's by design. Excitement and I don't do well together. It brings out the worst in me.

Plus I've already had enough of the E word this week to last me a lifetime.

My stomach clenches at the memory I've been trying not to replay every waking minute since Saturday night.

What in the hell is wrong with me?

Women like the one I try to be don't act like that. I'm a math professor for God's sake. I'm supposed to be rational. Careful. Calculating.

And maybe I am. Two of those anyway.

"Hey, Kerr."

I cringe at the sound of Nelson's voice behind me, then I plaster on a polite smile and turn to face the ex that won't quit.

"Hi." It sounds short and I feel bad. Nelson isn't a bad guy. Necessarily. He's polite and consistent and respectful. Perfectly acceptable. Like vanilla ice cream or sensible shoes. I force more warmth to my smile and my voice. "How are you doing?"

He tucks his hands into the pockets of his pressed slacks and nods his head. "You know I'm doing all right." He rocks onto the balls of his leather loafer wearing feet. "I've been doing a lot of soul searching with Dr. Gordon and I think I know what you needed from me that I didn't give you."

I lift a brow. "You do?"

I'm pretty sure Dr. Gordon has no clue what I need from a man. Some days I have a hard time admitting what I need from a man. Mostly because what I need and what I know I should want are two drastically different things.

Nelson pulls one hand free of his pocket and holds it out because talking without using his hands is next to impossible for him. Which is weird since he teaches public speaking classes. "I think you needed me to be stronger."

"Huh." That might have been the understatement of the century. "I would say that is an accurate statement." One that he's definitely heard before because it came out of my mouth like a hundred times over the course of our six month relationship. Hopefully he didn't pay Dr. Gordon too much for that revelation.

Nelson brightens, showing off his perfectly white, perfectly straight teeth with a wide smile the situation doesn't warrant. "See? So that's good right?"

"I guess so." I turn back to my desk and start going through the first pile of wayward papers. Monday's papers. I flip them into the recycling bin one by one as Nelson comes into my office and sits at my desk.

"Then let's go out for dinner Friday." He leans back in the seat, ready to get comfortable in my life. I've got news for him. I'm not even comfortable in my life. Not right now. Right now it feels like a wool sweater making me itchy and irritable.

And he's the matching scarf wrapped around my neck.

"I don't think so." I finish off Monday's stack and end up with only one paper for my keep pile. I tell myself I feel a little better already as I slip the single paper into the plastic organizer at the corner of the wide desk.

Nelson gapes at me, clearly surprised by my refusal. "But I had a breakthrough." He stands up from my chair and comes around the desk to place his hands on my shoulders. They're gentle and cool as they rest on the thin silk of my blouse. Nothing like the rough, strong hands I should never have let touch me the way they did Saturday night. Not because I didn't want Tracker to touch me.

But because of how much I did. In spite of who he is.

The clamminess of Nelson's hands on my shoulders drags me back to the task at hand. His eyes are pleading as they look into mine. "I've been trying, Kerr. I swear."

How in the hell did I get here? Apparently I was a little too easy when I cut Nelson loose two months ago. I try to be careful with what I say and how I say it which resulted in a break-up conversation that was a whole lot of it's-not-you-it's-me.

But it was all him.

I take a deep breath and stifle the side of me that wants to tell him the cold hard truth. The same side of me I wish didn't exist. Maybe if it didn't I would have found Nelson to be an acceptable companion.

Ew.

"I just don't think we are compatible." I slide out from under his touch easily and slip my shoes back on my feet. I need to get away from him right now before I say something harsh. We still have to work together and I can't handle him crying every time we pass in the hall.

Like he did after the first time we had sex.

And the second.

"I think it's time for you to move on and find someone who will appreciate you the way you deserve to be appreciated." I'm a little proud of that one. I give myself a mental pat on the back.

"But I want you."

It's a whine. He's whining. It makes my nose scrunch up like I smell something sour. This is why we can't be together. Because I want a man. Someone strong who takes what he wants and that includes me.

I just have to figure out how to make sure that situation doesn't bring out the worst in me. The side of me that can be ruthless. Reckless. Wild.

A little crazy.

Like it did Saturday.

I grab my leather work bag and toss it over my shoulder. "I'm sorry Nelson but I just don't think we want the same things." I grip the door to my office with one hand. "I have to go. I have someplace I have to be." I look at him and then

hair in at work. "I want you to go live your life and be happy."

Nelson's eyes widen almost to the point they're popping out of their head and he steps back, putting his hands up like he's expecting me to punch him. "I don't want any trouble."

I snag a bit of my wayward hair that's caught in my mouth with one finger and squint at him. "What in the hell are you talking about?"

I've been nothing but scarily polite to the guy, even when I wanted to scream at him and tell him to grow a pair and start acting like he has a dick. Never once did I do it because I can't let myself be like my father.

A heavy hand grips my elbow. "I've been looking for you."

I recognize the deep smooth voice immediately. I hate that it makes my thighs clench together as it drags the memory I've been avoiding all week to the forefront of my mind.

Nelson is still backing up, nearly tripping over his feet as he rushes to put more distance between him and the man holding me like he owns me.

I glare at my ex as he turns and rushes to his car without so much as a screw you I hope he kills you for dumping me. I take a deep breath before I turn my glare to the man beside me. "How do you know where I work?" I yank at my elbow but he holds fast.

"I know everything about you." He steps close to me, using his hold on my arm to keep me in place as his tall, broad body moves in, blocking out everything around us. "Including the face you make when you come, remember?"

Heat pricks across my skin and I tell myself it's from anger and not embarrassment. In reality it's neither of those things that's making me burn. I stare up at Tracker hoping he can't see what he does to me. "Then maybe you can do me a favor and tell my father I said fuck off."

I know who Tracker is. I knew the minute I saw the tattoo on his neck he was one of my father's men. I also knew he wasn't so sure who I was. To be honest I was a little insulted he'd think I was the kind of woman who'd dance on a table for attention.

Of course I did worse than that as a diversion.

Yup. A diversion. That's all it was between us in the bathroom. It had nothing to do with the fact that Tracker kissed me with more passion than Nelson worked up in six whole months. Combined.

I try again to pull free of his hold on my arm, aggravated with him for being here and myself for letting things go as far as they did at the bar. "Let me go."

"Nope. Not again. You and I need to have a talk and I'm not spending the next three days hunting your ass back down." He starts walking to the parking lot and goes directly to my friend's car. The one I'm driving instead of my own.

Because I'm not as stupid as he thought I was.

Unfortunately he's not as dumb as I was hoping either.

Tracker jostles me to a stop beside the passenger side. "Unlock it."

I tip my head back and stare him down, letting that difficult side of me creep into my tone. "No." The faster this man realizes what I am and what I can be, the sooner he will be begging off whatever job my father sent him here to do.

"Would you like for me to bust the window out then, Princess?" His hazel eyes don't wander from mine. My heart skips a beat at the heat lingering in their smoky depths. His nostrils flare and he tears his gaze from mine, snapping it to my best friend's car. "I think Shelly might have a bit of a problem with you bringing her car back with a broken window."

I shove my tongue against the roof of my mouth forcing away the urge to gulp. He knows more about my life than I expected. More than he should, which is nothing. Now the heat pumping through my veins is from anger. I lower my voice and narrow my eyes. "Stay away from Shelly."

I should never have asked her to help me. I know what my father is capable of, and attractive as this man is, he is probably just like King. No matter what, he is part of the world I never wanted to see again. The life I worked like hell to leave behind me. And I thought I had.

But the man standing here doing his best to intimidate me says different.

He steps closer. I can smell the spicy cologne I couldn't forget if I tried. It was pressed into my favorite dress as if it was a part of the fabric and still lingers in my closet at home. Tracker lowers his head and his voice. "Unlock. The. Door."

I plant my feet on the asphalt intending to stand my ground.

He raises his hand. I resist the urge to flinch, expecting the swing to come my way. Then I see the glass breaker in his fist.

"Stop." I rush to find Shelly's keys in my work bag. "Just stop." I pull out the keys and press the button on the fob.

His lips barely quirk as he opens the door and motions for me to get inside. "Was that so hard?"

I slide into the seat giving him the dirtiest look I can muster. He might now about my life. Where I work. Who my friends are. But there is one thing Tracker doesn't know.

The kind of woman I am.

He doesn't have a clue how hard I can make whatever this is.

Tracker is going to regret the day he agreed to come find me. I'll make sure of it.

3

Tracker

I TRY TO CALM myself down as I drive to Kerri's apartment, taking out my anger on the steering wheel, strangling it with both hands. She sits silently in the seat beside me staring daggers into the side of my head. King's daughter hates my guts right now and I'm fine with that.

I expected it.

What I'm not fine with is the way her pussy of a boyfriend looked at me. Like I was a thug. A

And it smells good. Like she just baked fucking cookies in the oven.

It feels like a home.

I've never lived in a place like this. I never will live in a place like this and I'm going to enjoy it while I can.

"You haven't told me anything." Kerri juts her hip out and fists her hand against it. "All you've done is show up and be a pain in my ass for no reason other than my father told you to."

"I did tell you, Princess." I drag the last word out to piss her off because I like it when she's mad. I stand up and walk toward her. "In the bathroom." I stop just in front of her. "Right before I made you come."

I see the heat flash across her eyes and it brings me an inordinate amount of satisfaction. Kerri liked what I did to her. Still likes the thought of it even though she doesn't want to.

"Why do you keep bringing that up?" Her voice is missing the edge it had a minute ago and a pink flush creeps up her neck.

I ease a little closer. She doesn't back up. "It's a fond memory." I breathe in the air around her. Spring. Fresh air and flowers. It soothes me in a way I don't want to think about so I decide to answer her question without making her ask again. As a show of good faith. "You are right. Your daddy sent me here."

"Why?"

Kerri still hasn't backed up so I press closer. Our bodies are almost touching now and my fingers twitch with the need to feel the soft curve of her hip in my grip. To add heft to the words I'm about to say. "To protect you."

Her eyes drop to my mouth for just a second. She licks her lips. "From?"

"King tried to take over a territory that didn't belong to..." I hesitate to use the word *us*. I'm a part of the club her daddy presides over but it isn't as comfortable of a fit as it used to be. I don't agree with the risks he's taking and I was mad as fuck he sent me away to babysit his daughter at a time like this.

I'm not as mad about that at this moment.

And that's why I'm struggling to tie myself to the man she clearly despises. I settle on the collective. "The Knights."

I keep going with my explanation. Maybe if Kerri understands what's going on it will make this whole situation go a hell of a lot smoother. "The club the territory belonged to has a problem with what happened and threatened to come after you and your momma."

The smooth set of her jaw softens. "Is my mom okay?"

I nod and file the bit of information she gave me away. Kerri might hate her daddy but her momma's a whole different story. "She's fine and she'll stay fine."

Kerri takes a long slow breath and blows it out. "I don't understand how this is happening." She turns and walks down the hallway, disappearing into her bedroom. "It's not like they know where I live."

"They'll find you. You know that." I listen as fabric rustles in the room a few steps away. I can imagine the reflection of her body in the full

48

length mirrors on the closet doors as she shucks her work clothes.

I shove my hand down my pants and adjust my stiff shaft. Why couldn't she be ugly? Or a prude?

That's the problem. One of many actually. After seeing the heat in her eyes when I brought up our time together Saturday night I know I can touch her again if I play my cards right. Which I will.

Kerri steps into the hall.

Fuck me.

I don't have to imagine her body anymore.

She's wearing just her panties and bra. They're pale pink lace. I don't even pretend not to look. I drink her in, letting my eyes slowly work their way down her frame. If she's going to put it out there I'm going to take it. Kerri's magnificent. Her hips and breasts are full and lush with a delicate curve pulling in at her waist.

"So you're here in case they find me?" She stands there like it's no big deal but I can tell by

life out of you because you've outgrown them to the point there's no way to force yourself to fit inside the seams anymore.

"Evan." It comes out easy. Too easy. "My name's Evan."

Violet works her jaw like she's mulling it over. She gives me a sharp nod. "It's a good name for a handsome boy." She pats my cheek and gives me a quick smile then pulls her hand away to point in the direction Butch just drove off on his hog. "Just don't interrupt my soaps with that bullshit and we'll get along fine."

I chuckle. "I will do my best."

She gives me one last look before turning to her door. I watch Violet go back inside and listen to make sure she locks the deadbolt. As I turn to sit on the stoop and wait for Butch to return with the car I catch the rustle of blinds in Kerri's front window. I smile as I drop to my ass on the cement and lean back against the door. Princess is in for a rude awakening if she thinks sleeping in a car is the worst she can do to me.

Spending the night in a car is nothing when you've slept on the streets.

Now, making me sleep beside her naked without touching her?

That would be a fucking nightmare.

Hopefully Kerri's not that creative.

Wait.

Maybe I take that back.

4

Kerri

"I WILL FIGURE something out." I tuck my cell phone between my shoulder and cheek as I stuff the hem of my blouse into the fitted waistband of my favorite navy blue pencil skirt. "Don't worry."

Shelly sighs into the phone. "Let's just reschedule. Wait until the situation is gone."

That's what we've been calling him. The situation.

"I can handle him." I slide on my pumps and check in the mirror on my closet door to make sure everything is in its place. "Just trust me. I promise I know how to handle this guy."

That was a complete lie. I had no idea how in the hell to handle Tracker.

Evan.

I shouldn't call him that. It makes me want to think of him as something he's not instead of what he is.

One of my father's men.

A biker.

An outlaw biker. The kind who likes to call the shots and run the show.

I run my own damn show.

"Well, if you can't make it I'll understand." I can hear the disappointment in Shelly's voice.

Today is my best friend's birthday and I'll be damned if I'm going to miss it because Ev— Tracker says I can't go out alone. He doesn't think it's safe and I'm sure as hell not taking him so that leaves me one option.

Make sure he doesn't notice I'm gone.

"I will make it and it will be awesome." I grab my work bag off the table and flip off the lights in my apartment. "I've got to go. I'll call you later." I almost hang up. "Wait." I stop and smile into the phone. "Happy birthday, Friend."

Shelly laughs. "Thank you. See ya."

Shelly has been my best friend since I met her in grad school. By then I was far enough away from the life I used to live that it was easier to talk about. She knows everything about me. What my father is. How he treated me like the son who probably would have appreciated the name Kerosene. Taking me under his wing and teaching me about life in the club. How to survive and run with the roughest crowd there is.

Then I grew tits and an attitude. After that I was useless to him. Unless of course I wanted to marry one of his men and learn how to be a proper kept woman. A shell with no opinion. No desires outside of serving her man and shutting her mouth.

Puke.

I'm sure I was one hell of an embarrassment to him. I'm sure it made The Knights question him as their leader when I took off. If a man struggling to forget what he did to me with his fingers and left wondering what Evan could accomplish with the rest of his body. It's all I can think about and now I'm even more sexually frustrated then I was before.

Which is what got me into this mess in the first place. It's why all my plans involving Tracker have more to do with how to get him closer to me than making him go back to where he came from which is what I should want. It's what I say I want.

But what I really want is becoming problematic. It's making me crazy.

And I've worked too hard to prove I'm not crazy.

But I'm not making any more mistakes. I'm going to do what needs to be done and deal with 'the situation'. Tonight I am going out, having fun, and pretending my father and Tracker don't exist.

Or at least half of those things.

Tracker pulls into my spot in the faculty lot at the back of the university. He turns to study me, his brows pushed together over the dark black of his sunglass. "What do you teach?"

"Math." I unlock my seatbelt. He's still staring at me.

"What sort of math?"

"The kind with numbers." I grab my bag and move to open the door but he's out his side and clicking the fob to keep me in the car until he reaches my side. He does it every damn time and I'd be lying if I said I hated it.

I wish I could find something I hated about him.

Besides that he's a Knight.

He opens my door and eyes me thoughtfully. "Numbers."

"That's what I said." I climb out of my seat and straighten my skirt. "And yes there is math without numbers."

"I know that." He shuts the door behind me as I stare at him.

I think he's serious.

Tracker holds one arm toward the building, motioning for me to lead the way. I want to ask if

65

to spring up and make me do things I shouldn't to get what I want.

And it was about to do it again.

I hurry to my office and drop my things on the desk before rushing down the hall to catch one of my pupils from last year as he leaves class. The kid's a brilliant student and also a decent pusher.

The latter is the reason for my interest in him this morning.

"Hey, Carson." I catch the tall skinny nineteen-year-old just as he leaves one of my fellow professor's rooms. He's a clean cut sophomore. You'd never guess he was one of the biggest dealers on campus. "I need a favor."

His gaze sweeps up and down the hallway. "Are you coming onto me, Ms. Wallace?"

That's how that came across? "Um. No." I take a step back just in case. I'm not into boys, especially of the student variety. Some of my contemporaries are happy to blur the lines. I'm not.

Sexually anyway. This is different. This is...

Me being in control of my life. It makes me feel better to think of it that way.

"I need some of your product."

His brows went up. "I have no idea what you're talking about."

I'm aggravated he is willing to consider fucking me but not selling to me. "Cut the shit, Carson. I'm not an idiot." Actually I am the farthest thing from an idiot when it comes to dealing drugs. That's the family business after all. "I want some glitter."

His brows come together in confusion. "You mean sparkle?"

Condescending little shit. He knows what the fuck I meant. "I want the stuff that makes you forget all your worries and responsibilities."

I know it's what all the kids here use on weekends to unwind. I'd overheard more than a few talking about it. Apparently it was the best way to escape life and get a good night's sleep.

And that's what I want for Tracker. I'm generous like that.

Carson shakes his head. "I don't do stuff like that."

Well damn. I was hoping he'd make this easy for me but it looks like I am going to have to be a bitch about it. "Don't make me fuck up your life, Carson." I glance down the hall to make sure we're alone. "All it takes is one phone call and they'll have dogs all over that nice apartment of yours."

His eyes widen.

I smile at him.

Carson pulls a tiny baggie of clear granules out of his pocket. He slips it into my hand.

"How much do I owe you?" I hold it up and eyeball the contents.

"Jesus." He shoves my hand down. "Don't hold it up." Carson steps back. "Just take it."

I roll my eyes as he quick steps away. It's like he thinks I've never done this before. I stop in my tracks.

He probably does. That is the point of every decision I've made since walking away from my father and his world.

Leaving that life behind.

I run my thumb across the bag in my hand. The one I just threatened a kid to get.

Well fuck.

I go back to my office trying to think of enough reasons why this is different to make me feel better. When I get there my phone dings as I walk through the door. It's a message from Shelly.

I made reservations for five at the restaurant. I hope everything is still on. Call me.

This is why it's different. I'm not trying to make money for a corrupt organization. I'm not hurting anyone. If anything Tracker will enjoy his evening. He won't have to worry about me or the suspiciously absent club that wants to hurt me.

And he'll get to sleep in a bed.

It's a win-win situation.

Yup. This is the right thing to do.

I am not like my father.

So I've done a few crazy things in the past few days. They were all for the greater good. To keep the life I've built for myself. A life far away from the world where my father controls everything and everyone.

That's why I need to cut the invisible tether that keeps pulling me toward Tracker. He might be sexy. He might be the kind of man I find difficult to resist. But I have to do it. Because every step I take closer to Evan is also a step closer to the life I swore I would never live again.

5

Tracker

I STARE AT her. I shouldn't be shocked, but I am. And it's not Kerri that shocked me. I did it to myself. I almost forgot what I am.

And what I'm not.

"I wasn't going to use it." She stares at the pile of crap that up until a few minutes ago was packed into her work bag. Now it's dumped on the table so I can see what else she plans to use against me. "Why were you going through my bag anyway? You haven't taken over enough of my life?"

"Taken over you're—" I don't even know what to say to her at this point. If Kerri thinks making sure she doesn't get kidnapped and hurt, probably even worse, is taking over her life then we are on two totally different pages. "I am trying to make sure you don't end up fucking dead and you are making it nearly impossible to do that."

She has tried to get away from me every fucking day. Climbing out windows, sneaking through unmarked exits at work, calling her friends to pick her up blocks away. Kerri is the first person I've ever not been able to keep track of. She's defiant. She's headstrong. She's wild. And as much as I love all those traits in a woman they're making it hell on me right now and if I mess this up she's the one who'll suffer.

That's when I realize. I can't protect this woman. She won't let me.

"What exactly were you planning to do tonight?" I hold up the tiny clear plastic baggie I found in her work bag. The contents are a new designer drug popular with the younger, higher-end crowd. I look through the bag at her. "Did you think fucking dust would be able to take me down?"

"I wasn't trying to take you down." She starts picking up the shit I dumped out of her bag and shoving it back into place.

If Kerri hadn't been such a pain in the ass today I never would have searched in there. I just can't trust her. She's going to get herself hurt trying to prove she's the boss and I needed to know what else she had up her sleeve.

Now I know.

And I wish I didn't because it's left me no choice. I grab her arm. "Come on." I drag her out the door and to her car, practically throwing her in the front seat. She doesn't try to get out like normal while I go to the driver's side. When I get in, she's rubbing her arm where I held her. I try to ignore the guilt that tugs at me.

I didn't mean to hurt her.

That's why I'm doing this. Because if she stays with me she's going to get hurt and I don't want that to happen. I promised I would do whatever it took to protect her and I'm going to keep my promise. Not because of King.

Because of her.

Kerri needs protecting. I'm more certain of this now than ever. She's her own worst enemy and all she wants to do is fight me every step of the way. Any other time I would be up for the battle.

But not when her safety is at risk.

"Where are we going?" Her voice is flat. "You can't just take me to some safe house and lock me up."

"We're not going to a safe house." I speed out of town. There's no safe house that could hold this woman.

She sits silent in the seat as we make the drive to the last place on Earth she wants to go. I don't want to take her here but I have no clue what else to do. I have to take her home.

As we near the town where she grew up and her daddy rules the streets Kerri sits up straight in her seat, her wide eyes staring out the windows as she twists to look out every one. She's figured it out.

"No." She shakes her head. "Please don't do this to me."

"You didn't give me any other option." I pull into the driveway of her daddy's expensive house and let her jump out of the car.

She's easy to catch as her high heels dig into the grass on the neighbor's manicured front yard. I pick her up, kicking and screaming, and throw her over my shoulder.

"Evan, please. I'm sorry. Just take me home. I promise I'll be good."

She uses my real name. It puts a hitch in my step as I walk up the sidewalk of the house she grew up in. I hate to do this to her but I can't trust her and I sure as hell can't keep her safe. King needs to find someone else.

I ring the doorbell.

Her momma answers the door with her daddy two steps behind. When King sees me he smiles. "Hell yeah. It's about time a man showed that girl how things are."

Mrs. Wallace steps aside and I walk into the open foyer of the giant house, dropping Kerri to her feet. "I'm sorry but I don't think I'm the man for this job."

Kerri's eyes don't go near her daddy. She stands tall, her lips pressed together so tight they're white. Her momma rushes to hug her.

"Honey, I've missed you so much."

"Stop making a fool of yourself, woman." Kerri's dad grabs his wife by the shoulder and pulls her back roughly. "Act right."

Mrs. Wallace immediately nods, her chocolate brown eyes on the ground. They're Kerri's eyes only without the fire burning behind them.

King snuffed that out long ago.

I look back at Kerri.

I shouldn't have done this.

I just wanted to keep her safe.

Her daddy glowers at me. "Of course you're the man for the job." He snorts at his daughter. "This one here has been nothing but a pain in my ass almost her whole damn life. Won't listen for shit." His nostrils flare. "Doesn't know a woman's place."

I can almost see her wilting under his hard glare. The strength she shows me in spades shrinking to nothing in his smothering presence.

I knew King was a bad guy. I knew he did bad things to other bad men. But this man that I'm seeing right now is so much worse than I ever could have imagined.

King is a monster.

He steps up to her and grabs her face, shoving her chin up, forcing her to look him I the eye. "You listen to me. Tracker is in charge of you. He's says jump, you say how fuckin high."

"No."

The word comes out of her mouth strong and clear as a tiny bit of the Kerri I'm used to seeing creeps back in.

Her daddy pulls back a hand. She flinches, ready for the impact.

It's not coming.

I promised I would protect Kerri from anyone who tried to hurt her and that includes the prick in front of me.

I stare at the man who gives me orders, his wrist tight in my grip. I don't take my eyes off him as I tip my head toward his daughter. "Kerri. Go get in the car."

Her daddy smirks as he turns to me. "Hold on a minute, Princess." He eyes me like a bug under a microscope. "If I find out you get away from Tracker here again," he turns his glare to Kerri, "he's going to be the one who suffers for it."

King yanks his hand free, his eyes cold and hard as they focus on mine. "Now get the fuck out of my house."

I push Kerri out the door ahead of me. She lets me guide her to the car and put her inside. We're almost home before I trust myself to speak. "I'm sorry. I didn't know he treated you like that."

She stares out the windshield. "How could you not know?"

It's hard to explain how I live with being what I am. That the only way I can do what I do is to put on blinders to what's happening around me. I have to. Joining the club wasn't a choice for me.

It was a necessity.

I only just started to see King for what he was. How he manipulates his position to get what he wants from the Knights that idolize him. I know he's a bad guy when it comes to dealing with men, but being a criminal and being an abusive piece of shit to your own flesh and blood are two different things.

"I keep my head down, Kerri. I do what I'm told and I try to go on." I have a skill King needs. I can find anyone. Anywhere. Anytime. It's that same skill that landed me where I am right now. Struggling to do right by the woman beside me.

I risk a glance Kerri's way just as her fingers brush across her cheek.

She's crying.

And I'm a piece of shit. I just proved everything everyone has ever thought of me and more.

I want to drive back and give her daddy what he deserves for doing this to her, doing this to me, but that would be suicide for at least one of us. "I wish you told me why you left."

"It doesn't matter." She sniffs.

I pull into her apartment's lot and park in her spot. I turn to her. "It does matter." A damp tear streak glistens on her cheek. I want to wipe it away but I don't. Instead I get out of the car and go to her door. She lets me open it without locking me out. I hold my hand out to her.

It's a peace offering. I don't know if she'll take it as that but I'm offering it anyway. I don't want to fight with her. I just want to make sure she's as perfect when I leave as she was when I got here.

That's all.

Kerri looks at my hand. Then at me. "Is my father going to hurt you for what I did?"

I should lie to her but I won't. I need her to realize how serious this is. "I don't know." King will most likely punish me for what happened today and I will deserve everything he dishes out for what I just did to his daughter.

Kerri barely nods. Then she puts her hand in mine and I pull her out of the car, tucking her under my arm. I lead her to the door and open it, shucking my boots before I step inside. She stands by the door quietly as I check the apartment. It's clear.

Her phone starts to ring on the table beside me as I walk past the dining area. I pick it up and carry it to her. "It's Shelly."

She slides her finger across the screen and answers. "Hey. I'm sorry for the late notice but we have to reschedule." Her brown eyes slide across the room until they land on me. "Yeah." She disappears down the hall.

I walk back to the door and start to slip my boots back on.

"Wait."

I turn around. She's standing in the hall. For the first time since I've met her Kerri looks uncertain.

"I'm sorry." She crosses the living room and stops right in front of me. "I just..." She shakes her head and blinks her eyes. "I hate him. I hate what he is." Her voice is quiet and soft but her words still cut me. It's what I know is true. I know how people look at me, how *she* looks at me, but hearing it still guts me.

"And I proved I'm as bad as he is." If Kerri's a lamb then tonight I led her to slaughter. I might have stepped in and stopped it, but the damage is done. I tried to pretend King and I could be separate in her eyes but we can't. We are one and the same to her and I cemented that belief tonight.

Kerri's head tips back quickly. "What? No." She shakes her head. "You're nothing like him." She lays her hands on my chest. "That's why I'm sorry. What happened tonight is my fault. I pushed you too far and I'm sorry. Sometimes I'm just—" Her voice trails off.

84

The heat of her palms soaks into my skin through the fabric of my shirt, warming me in an odd way. "I just want to keep you safe, P—" I catch the word before it comes out. "Kerri."

"I know." Her hands slide up higher, over my collarbone and across my shoulders. Her body moves closer. She gazes up at me, her lashes long and dark as they move with her eyes, studying my face. Her hands slide over the skin of my neck, the pads of her fingers tracing the lines inked into my flesh. "Your artwork is beautiful."

I've never had anyone call a single part of me that word before.

"Thank you." I can't stop watching Kerri and I'm sure as hell not going to stop her from touching me. Not yet.

"Is there more?" Her eyes move down, over the rest of me.

"Yes."

One hand runs down my arm, skating over the skin covered by a full sleeve of dark, twisted images. It's the first work I had done. When I was young and angry at what life handed me. Or didn't hand me.

Kerri hooks her arm around my neck and pulls up on her toes. Her breath whispers across my lips. "I want you to stay here tonight." She brushes her lips against mine in a kiss that's very different from the first one we shared. It's soft and sweet. Like I think she might have been if her life was different.

Kerri pulls back and looks up at me, her eyes dark and hooded. "With me."

It's an offer no man in his right mind would refuse.

I'm going to anyway.

"I'm happy to stay inside but all you're going to be doing this evening is sleeping."

I hold in a smile as the fire I missed seeing flashes through her eyes.

She drops her feet flat to the ground. "I just offered to fuck you."

"And I politely declined."

Kerri gives me one shouldered shrug. "Fine then. Sleep in your car." She spins and starts to walk away.

She doesn't make it far. I grab her and pull her soft warmth against me. "I wasn't done." I slide my hands down her body as I press it into mine. "I declined for tonight." I cup her bottom, squeezing the fullness of her ass as I drop to run my lips along her neck. "I will fuck you Kerri, but it will be when I decide." I suck on her earlobe. The soft gasp she lets out satisfies me on an uncomfortably deep level. "Not when you want to distract yourself."

Her body is hot where it meets mine, stoking the desire that's been eating me alive since the night I met her. All I want is to watch her come for me again. Hear her call my name.

But tonight is not the time. Not for me and certainly not for her.

Kerri lets out a long sigh and relaxes against me. "I'm hungry."

I can't fix her dad. I can't help her mom. I can't take back the mistake I made tonight and I can't do anything to change the past.

Hers or mine.

But this I can fix. Tonight I can take care of her. I owe it to her.

That and a lot more.

I cup her face in my hands and gently press my lips to her forehead. "I'll order dinner."

She gives me a small smile. "I wasn't really going to make you sleep in your car."

I raise an eyebrow at her. "Yes you were."

Her mouth opens.

I lift her chin with my finger.

"I'd have made me sleep in my car too."

6

Kerri

"HOW DO YOU keep getting fresh clothes?" I look Evan up and down as he walks out of my spare bedroom, buttoning the cuff of his shirt. His eyes lift from his wrist to settle on mine and my heart skips a beat.

Stupid thing.

It's just because he fills out his suit so well. That's all. Any woman would struggle around a man like Evan.

"My roommate has been helping me out." He finishes up with his cuff and pulls on his suit jacket, stretching his long arms into the sleeves before tugging at the lapels to work it into place over the open-neck crisp white shirt he's wearing. Just like the night we met.

Evan gives me a wink. "He was also nice enough to make sure I was fed and clothed during my camp out."

Guilt twists my stomach.

He put himself on the line for me yesterday. Even after I've given him every reason not to, he protected me just like he said he would. I never imagined that would come to include my father. Standing up to the club president isn't something a member does.

Not if he wants to keep living life like he normally does. As a member.

With all his teeth.

He smiles at me, showing off the straight white line of teeth I'd hate to see damaged because of me. "You clean up nice, Numbers."

I'm wearing a fitted black dress that hugs my curves. Like the one I wore the night he couldn't keep his hands off me because...

Just because.

"You've moved on from Princess?" I think I'm teasing him but the darkness that clouds his eyes tells me Evan didn't take it as a joke.

"I won't call you that word again." His jaw is tight as he stares at me. I watch the slow rise and fall of his chest as he breathes. It's the only move he makes for a long time. Long enough it makes me jump when he starts to walk toward me.

Evan freezes. His head tips slightly to one side and I almost think I see a flash of hurt in his eyes. "Are you afraid of me, Kerri?"

I laugh because that is the most ridiculous thing he's ever said. "You?" I walk toward him, eating up the rest of the distance between us to prove the answer I'm about to give him. "No. Not even a little."

"Really?" He watches me as I continue to close the gap separating us. "Not even a little?"

I don't stop until I'm pressed against him. "Not even a little."

He slept in the bedroom next to mine last night and I'm a little annoyed by it. I've never made an offer like I made him last night and been refused, but Evan turned me down. Flat.

I won't let him turn me down tonight.

I want to see how it feels to be with someone like him. A man who is strong and aggressive and dominant.

But different.

It's not a good idea. I know it. But if I don't find out I'll wonder the rest of my life.

It will be fine. I can do this as long as I don't lose control of the situation. I simply have to make sure I don't get attached to Tracker because even if he is different, even if he isn't like my father...

He's still one of them.

And I worked too hard to get away. I can't look back. No matter how nice the view is.

But I want to know what it's like to be with a man as strong as I am. One who pushes back but doesn't try to crush me. Break me the way my father broke my mother.

Evan's hands rest on my hips. They slide around to cup my ass and I can feel my pulse pick up as he runs his fingers over the full curve of my cheeks to tuck against the juncture of my thighs, stopped from going any farther by the fabric of my dress. He's never shied away from touching me. He doesn't ask permission and he doesn't hesitate. I like that. I like that he takes what he wants.

Even if I try to give him more.

"I bet your friends will feel differently." I see a hint of uncertainty on his face and it makes me question if I've already lost control of what's happening between us.

I shove the thought away. I am a strong fucking woman. If I don't want a man for anything other than to satisfy my curiosity then that's how it will be. I will not develop feelings for him.

I mean I was with Nelson six months and didn't end up with any feelings besides pity for the guy.

I can do this my way. Just like I've done everything else in my life. I am in control. I run this show and that includes my decisions and my emotions.

I straighten his lapels. "You might be surprised."

If Tracker thinks my friends are going to be intimidated by the way he looks then he's about to have an enlightening evening. Maybe it will be good for him.

He snaps one arm out, forcing the sleeve of his jacket above his watch. He looks at the timepiece that probably cost more than my rent. It's another reminder of the life he lives.

The same life I will never go back to. Or even within spitting distance of.

The money is good if you're in the right position and from the cut of his suit and the watch on his wrist, Tracker is an indispensable part of the club and my father compensates him accordingly. But that only means his life there is set. My father wouldn't let him go, even if he wanted to leave.

Jesus.

I take a step back. Shit. I just wondered if Tracker would consider leaving the club. I need a little space between us.

I plaster a smile on my face as panic pumps through my veins. "Are you ready?"

"Always." Tracker grabs my car keys off the table and opens the door for me, reminding me how many potential problems there are with my plan to keep my feelings for him on a strictly physical level.

Problem number one. He's chivalrous.

I give him a tight smile as I walk through the open door and outside into the waning evening sun. I hear the deadbolt lock and within seconds his hand is at my elbow, guiding me to the car.

Where he opens the door.

I slide into the seat and buckle up as he shuts the door and walks to the other side. I watch as Tracker scans the area as he moves, giving the neighborhood one last look before getting into the driver's seat.

It's been at least a week since he was assigned to watch out for me and nothing has happened. Not a single threat to my safety.

Except the time I shimmied out a bathroom window in a skin tight dress to get away from him. And the time I got lost trying to sneak away from him at work. And the time I jumped into traffic trying to outrun him.

It's no wonder he thought taking me to my father was his only option.

It was.

"Where are we going?" Evan backs out of my assigned parking spot and pulls into the narrow driveway that runs between each of the large brick apartment buildings lining my street.

"The Italian Oven." I point to the left. "It's about ten minutes away."

That's the good thing about living in a college town. Anything I want is almost within walking distance. Food. Alcohol. Shopping. I never have to venture too far from home if I don't want to.

He turns out of the lane and onto the narrow unmarked street. The sidewalks are full of students walking. Probably enjoying the last of the school year before heading home to their families and going from independent living to being back under their parent's roof.

The car is quiet except for the two times I have to tell Evan which way to turn. I want to talk to him. I want to ask him a million questions about his life and his friends and his family. That's why I don't. Because the less I know about him the better. I don't need to know any of it and it will be easier for me if I don't.

Unless he has some terrible deep dark secret that would make it easy to hate him. That would be helpful right about now.

We pull into the busy lot behind The Italian Oven and I see Shelly's car parked. I start to get out, excited to see my best friend and have a glass of wine to help me relax. I pull on the handle. The locks click closed.

I sit back in my seat and wait for him. Evan opens the door. "I thought we were past that?"

I smile at him as I get out. "You thought wrong."

He rests his hand on the small of my back as we walk to the restaurant. His eyes never stop moving, watching everything happening around us. I wish I didn't like the way it makes me feel to have him beside me, watching out for me.

But it's just an order he's following.

It's not though. I can't even make myself pretend it is. If it was just that he'd have let my father slap me and probably consider it a favor. Hoping it would put me back in line and make me easier to handle.

"You all right?" Evan opens the door to the restaurant and the smell of garlic and baked cheese wafts out.

I nod. "Just hungry."

He uses his hand on my back to direct me inside. "Then I suppose it's a good thing we're in the right kind of place to remedy that."

I see Shelly right away because she stands up from the table we reserved for our group. There are normally three of us. Me, Shelly and her roommate Becca, but tonight Becca brought two girls she works with. I met them once and I liked the short one, Amber maybe? But the tall gorgeous one? Felicity?

She makes me want to gouge her eyeballs out with a spork.

But I won't because it's Shelly's party. And I love her. And she'd probably never speak to me again if I shed blood at her birthday dinner. Not to mention the extra charge The Italian Oven would add to our bill for body fluid removal.

"Hey!" Shelly runs toward me, teetering in her heels as she rounds the table. She grabs me in a tight hug. "I'm so glad to see you." She pulls back and goes for Tracker, wrapping her long, fair-skinned arms around him, bouncing a little as she squeezes him. "Thank you for taking care of my friend."

Shelly knows about what happened with my dad. Not just what went on yesterday, but what happened everyday growing up in my house. The way he treated me and my mom.

Still treats my mom.

She hugs Tracker for long enough he starts to look a little uncomfortable. Finally Shelly releases him and looks up at his face. "You are just the cutest thing."

She says it like he's a kitten or a puppy. Some adorable little furry creature instead of a very large, very intimidating looking biker.

Becca grabs Shelly's arm. "Sit down. We're getting ready to order."

A waitress is standing at the end of the table looking at us impatiently. Shelly grabs my hand and pulls me around the table with her. "You guys can sit beside me. I want to hear more about you, Evan."

Tracker looks at me when she calls him by name. It's a strange look. One that I can't quite read.

Shelly sits down and I sit next to her. Tracker scoots my chair in for me before sliding into the one beside me. We order and the minute the waitress leaves Becca, Shelly's friend from high school and long time roommate, leans across the table. "Is he your boyfriend?"

Becca is a different sort of person. She's blunt. Very, very blunt. Everything is black or white for her. It either is, or it isn't. It wouldn't occur to her not to ask a question she wants the answer to, no matter how awkward or invasive.

But I like her anyway.

I turn to Tracker. "No." I look back at Becca, not really sure how to explain the situation. No one here knows what my family is besides Shelly. I don't like for people to know what I came from.

What I escaped.

Evan leans closer to me as he directs his attention to Becca. "I have to spend a little time in town for work and Kerri's been nice enough to take me in while I'm here." Evan's gaze stays on Shelly's roommate as he gives her the stretched-truth explanation. Becca's eyes are glued to him, watching his lips as every word passes through them.

"I'm Becca." She shoves her hand across the table at him.

Tracker takes her hand in a gentle but firm handshake. His eyes move to me for a split second then ease back to Becca. "Evan."

Becca doesn't miss a beat before hitting him with her next question. "Are you a biker?"

"I am." Tracker takes a sip of his water.

I watch him, looking for any sign of irritation with the extreme amount of attention he's getting but he only looks relaxed as Becca peppers him with questions about exactly how difficult it is to ride a motorcycle. Don't you feel like you're going to tip over when you go around a corner? Doesn't it get hot? Doesn't it get cold? She goes on and on listening intently to each patient answer before asking the next.

"God, Becca." Felicity rolls her glitter-shadow-covered eyes from where she sits on the other side of Evan. "He doesn't want to answer any more of your stupid questions."

Felicity angles her long, lithe body in Evan's direction, giving him an unobstructed view of the deep cleft between her breasts. "I have a question for you." She leans her chin against the knuckles of her left hand. "How many tattoos do you have?"

Evan shifts in his seat and I could swear he moves closer to me. "I've never counted."

That was a lie. I would bet all my money that man knew each and every tattoo that marked his body, including when he got it and what it meant. It's clear the tattoos on his body have a deep meaning to him. Unfortunately, based on the gnarled silhouettes and dark colors I would guess it's not happiness Evan was feeling when he got them.

Felicity's clear blue eyes travel down, raking over the man between us. "Well where all do you have them?"

Evan clears his throat.

I shove up from the table. "I need to go to the bathroom."

"I'll take you." Evan immediately stands beside me.

Felicity snorts. "That's ridiculous. If you're scared to go alone I'll go with you." She stands up.

Well shit. I give her a forced smile. "That's fine."

Either way I'm getting her away from Evan. Felicity's clearly making him uncomfortable and I owe him an ass-saving. It's not nearly the same level of ass-saving as what he did for me though.

Felicity's worse than my father could ever be.

We walk into the ceramic tiled bathroom and she stands in the mirror while I go in the stall and try to prove my need to be here. I manage to squeeze out a tinkle before siding up to her at the sink where she's applying a thick layer of extra shiny gloss to her lips.

"I'm not sure why you brought a man like that to dinner."

I turn on the water and start to wash my hands, counting to ten before I open my mouth. It's the first trick I learned when I realized I had a temper to control. "Why's that, Felicity?"

"I mean, you clearly like him and he's obviously not into you." She rubs her lips together and pushes her tits up higher in her dress. "I would think you'd be smart enough to know Evan would move on once he saw what else he could be spending his time doing while he's in town."

I'm going to have to kill her I think.

7

Tracker

I THINK SHE'S going to kill her.

"What in the hell is wrong with you?" The skinny brunette on my left looks at Kerri, eyes brimming with feigned innocence.

"With me?" Kerri's eyes go so wide I think they might pop out of her head. She points to the wad of satin in my lap. "You just dropped your panties in his lap."

"So?" The brunette whose name I can't remember shrugs her shoulder. "It's not like he wanted *your* panties in his lap."

A level of rage I've never seen flashes in Kerri's dark eyes.

Oh Shit.

I barely manage to grab her as she lunges across me, grabbing the panties as she goes. Kerri twists in my arms, trying to break free of my hold on her. She looks at me.

"Please let me go." Her voice is terrifyingly calm.

I pull her tighter against me. Partly to keep her from getting loose and partly because I like the feel of her stretched across my lap, especially while she's in a fit of jealous rage.

Over me.

I lean into her ear. "Not until you calm down."

"I am calm." That same low, slow voice that would make a rational person run like hell. "I just want to give Felicity her panties back."

I look down at the tiny garment clutched in her fist. I don't want to touch them. That's why they were still on my lap in the first place. But

I'm a grown-ass man and I promised I would protect Kerri from anyone who might hurt her.

So far nine times out of ten it's been from herself.

I pluck the panties from her hand, pinching them between two fingers, letting the rest dangle in the air as I pass them to their original owner. Felicity snatches them from my hand, her high-gloss lips curled into a snarl.

I would guess that means her offer's off the table.

"You don't have to wave them around like a flag." She shoves them in her purse with a huff. "I'm fucking leaving. This is ridiculous." She jumps up so fast her chair tips over. She snaps her fingers at the woman sitting beside her who hasn't spoken a word all night. "Come on. We're leaving."

The shorter woman jumps up and rushes to follow Felicity from the restaurant.

"Poor Amber." Shelly shakes her head. "She's so sweet when she finally gets a chance to talk but for some reason she won't go anywhere without that one."

Becca hasn't flinched during the whole panty ordeal. Just kept eating her spaghetti like everyone at the table was discussing taxes instead of borderline brawling. Now she puts her fork down and looks up. Her eyes wander down the table. "Where are Felicity and Amber?" She focuses on Kerri. "Why are you on his lap?"

I can feel Kerri start to relax. She looks at Becca for a second, then she starts to laugh. "Becca, I love you." She slides off my lap and back into her seat. "You missed all the fun. What in the world were you thinking about?"

Becca looks at Kerri like she should know. Her eyes flick to me and then back to Kerri. "Well, motorcycles of course."

Kerri laughs again. "Fair enough."

Becca turns to me. "Would you take me for a ride on yours sometime?"

I give her a grin. I like this girl. She doesn't pull any punches and for some reason finds what

I am fascinating. I don't usually get that. "I would love to."

"Have you been riding for a long time?" Shelly looks at me from her spot beside Kerri.

"As soon as I could afford a bike I bought one." It was an easy answer that didn't give too much away. The life I've lived isn't the kind of story people like to discuss over dinner. Or at all.

No one likes to hear there are some kids who grow up alone, ending up on the streets as their eighteenth birthday present because that's when the government isn't required to take care of them anymore.

Shelly studies me for a second. She glances to Becca who is completely focused on the screen of her cell phone. Her warm eyes come back to me. "Seriously. Thank you for taking care of my friend." She elbows Kerri. "Even though she's a pain in the ass."

I lean closer and wrap my arm around the back of Kerri's chair. It's hard to keep my hands off her right now. Not that it was easy before, but the minute she went after Felicity something changed. I smile at Shelly. "I was warned."

The waitress stops with a stack of checks, looking at the empty chairs. "Uh. Did they leave?"

"Well shit." Shelly looks across the table at Becca. "I was so happy to see her gone I didn't even think about that."

I take the checks from the young waitress and slide three hundreds into the top leather folder before handing it back to her. "No change."

I turn back to the table and Kerri is watching me. I pretend not to notice. Shelly has her purse on her lap and a credit card in her hand. She looks at the spot where the waitress stood a few seconds ago. "Where'd she go?"

"I took care of it." I slap on my Mr. Charming smile. "Consider it a birthday present and my penance for ruining girl's night."

Shelly snorts and shoots a dirty look at the empty end of the table. "You weren't the one who ruined girl's night." She turns to Becca. "Probably no more invites for Felicity."

Becca shrugs. "I never invite her. She just shows up."

I still have my arm across the back of Kerri's chair and I let my thumb stroke across the bare skin of her shoulder. I catch Shelly's eyes on the subtle caress. Her lips curve into a smile as she looks away.

"Well I think I might have had enough excitement for tonight." Shelly stands up and pulls her purse over her shoulder. "I'm going to have to take a rain check on drinks. I feel a carb coma coming on." She gives me a wink over Kerri's head.

Kerri stands up. "Are you sure?" She blows out a breath. "I'm sorry. I wasn't really going to try to shove her underwear down her throat."

I almost laugh out loud because if there's one thing I've learned about the woman beside me it's when she says she wasn't really going to do something...

She absolutely was.

"I would have helped you do it if I could've reached her." Shelly looks at me. "I'm sorry. We really are nice women I promise." She pushes past Kerri to pull me into another hug. "Thank you for dinner." She tips up on her toes and whispers in my ear. "Don't let her scare you off."

I don't have time to react to Shelly's comment before Becca jumps into my arms, hugging me tight. I feel her hands moving over my back. "You have really well-developed muscles." She drops back to her feet and pokes at my shoulders. "Do you exercise regularly?"

Such a strange little woman. "I do. It's important in my line of work."

"What is it you do?"

"Currently?" I fish for a decent term. "Personal protection."

"So, like a bodyguard?" Becca sounds entirely unimpressed.

"Yeah, like a bodyguard." I glance next to me at the body I'm currently required to guard. "It's not a bad gig."

Shelly snickers behind my back.

I walk the women to the parking lot, making sure Shelly and Becca are safely on their way before Kerri and I pull out of the lot. Kerri is quiet beside me, staring out the window.

"Everything okay?"

She nods. "I shouldn't have gone after her like that." I see her jaw set. "That woman just rubs me the wrong way. Makes me act like something I never wanted to be."

I feel sick to my stomach as the realization of what she means hits me. "You are nothing like him."

"That's not true." She crosses her arms at her waist. "I blackmailed a kid into giving me drugs. I sexually assaulted you in a bathroom and I one-hundred percent was going to make Felicity choke on her panties." She blinks hard. "I worked so hard to be different. Nothing like him or what he expected me to be."

"Kerri." I reach for her over the console. "Trust me when I say you are nothing like him. Everything you did was self-preservation. You considered me a threat to the life you have." I swallow back the tightness cinching my throat. "If I had the life you do I would fight for it too."

Her life is the kind of thing a person like me isn't supposed to even think about having. Nobody pays an orphan's way through school. No one pushes you to be better than you are. No one understands you want to be different than the life you came from. They expect nothing of you and as a result you expect nothing of yourself.

Because you are nothing.

"What about the part where I tried to asphyxiate a woman with a thong?" She looks at me and I see a little bit of the challenge returning to her eyes. "She's no threat to me."

"No. No she is not." Felicity might turn some men's heads but she wasn't my kind of girl. I like a strong woman as much as the next guy, but that one can cut fucking glass.

"I just don't understand who she thinks she is." Kerri starts mumbling under her breath. I only catch every other word or so but it's clear I was wrong before. Numbers isn't jealous.

She is *very* jealous.

I'm still smiling about it as I pull behind her apartment building. My smile fades instantly.

Scrawled across her door in messy red writing are two words that turn my blood to ice.

Found you

Kerri sits up straight in her seat. "Evan?"

I don't have time to enjoy hearing her call me by name. I pull out my cell and dial the only man in the world I've ever trusted. Butch picks up on the first ring.

"Yo. Girls made it home and everything looks good here."

He's been helping me since Kerri gave me the slip that first night. I knew then this wasn't a one man job.

I hate that I was right.

"I need you to come to Kerri's now." I turn the car around and drive back toward the exit, scanning the lot for any unknown vehicles. "We've got a problem."

"Where are we going?" Kerri looks out the back window as we drive away from her apartment.

I quickly pull back onto the road and speed away from her building. "We're going to make sure no one was sitting and waiting for us to come home." I should have paid better attention. I should have checked every fucking car we passed on the way home. But I didn't.

Because Kerri was upset and all I cared about was making her feel better.

And it could have ended badly for both of us.

I circle back around, checking every side street as we pass, making eye contact with every driver coming in the other direction. Looking. Sensing.

It's what makes me different. The best at what I do.

Usually.

Except apparently this time. Kerri's thrown me off from the first second. I need to change that. Right fucking now.

My phone rings.

"Yeah."

"That's not good." Butch's voice muffles but I can still hear him talking to Kerri's neighbor. "I understand Miss Violet, that's why I brought my car this time."

I hear Violet in the background, giving Butch hell about his car not being any less fucking loud than his bike. He must be in the Camaro. The muffled sounds stop and his voice comes back loud and clear again. "I don't see anything out here. I'm gonna talk to Miss Violet and see if she saw anything. Come on back."

I don't know if I feel better or worse. If whoever wrote on Kerri's door was still there I'd be able to send a message to the people threatening to hurt her. Let them know I won't allow them to use her as a pawn in whatever fucked up game we're playing.

But then Kerri would be reminded of what I am. The ties I have to the man she hates.

I hang up my phone.

"I didn't think it was real." The words are almost a whisper. I chance a look at her even though I know what I see will only make the anger burning inside me worse. Her skin is pale, the flush of color her cheeks carried since the incident with Felicity drained. Her hands are braced against the seat on either side of her thighs, as if she's ready to push off and run the minute I say go. She turns to look at me. "What in the hell are we going to do?"

We.

Not what are *you* going to do.

Not what am *I* going to do.

We.

I reach across and grab the hand closest to me. "We are going to be just fine." I pull her cold fingers to my mouth and run my lips across her knuckles. "I promise."

She swallows hard and nods.

She believes me. That means in some small way Kerri trusts me to take care of her. A part of me stirs. A part I never wanted to admit I had. The part of me that wanted to think I could have someone like her. That a woman like this would look at me as something other than a way to get her rocks off.

Something more.

I pull into her spot at the apartment and park. Butch is still standing by the door. It's clean. Not a trace of what was there only a few minutes ago. I open Kerri's car door and offer my hand. She takes it like she has the last few times only this time I don't let go. I hold her hand in mine as we walk across the lot to where Butch is taking a container of cookies from Violet.

She looks our way and gives me a bright smile. She touches her hair. "So many handsome men around here suddenly."

It's funny that it takes an old woman to make me blush. "How are you this evening, Violet?"

She opens her eyes wide and blows out a long sigh. "Well I don't even know now." She looks at Butch. "Anthony was asking me if I saw anything suspicious and then I saw Kerri's door and I don't even know what to think now."

Anthony. Looks like I'm not the only one with a soft spot for Violet.

Butch and I are similar men. Both in the club because we were men without a family looking for a place where we belonged. Society's lost boys.

The only difference is Butch found the club.

The club found me.

"Don't worry." I nod to Butch. "We'll make sure everything's okay."

Butch thumbs toward the bright yellow Camaro parked next to Kerri's sedan. "I'll be here all night."

I look at the car and then back at him. "Way to blend in."

Butch shrugs. "Doesn't matter much now, does it?"

They found her. All this time I was hoping it wouldn't happen. That it was an empty threat.

I knew better.

I clap Butch on the shoulder as I walk through Kerri's door. "Thanks man. Call me if you see anything."

He nods as I close the door behind us and lock the deadbolt.

Kerri walks across the carpet without taking off her shoes. She spins in a slow circle to face me. "Are we safe here?"

"We are for now. If that changes, we'll deal with it then."

She rubs her hands up and down her arms. She looks at the door. "So your friend has a key to my apartment too?"

I feel the tug of guilt for what I had to do to make sure Kerri was safe. We're taught in the club to do what we want without asking for permission but it's never been easy for me. "He does."

She nods.

"Do you want me to take it?" It would be a stupid thing to do, especially after what happened tonight, but I would. Kerri wanted to leave her father's world behind her and I brought it right to her doorstep.

And had keys made for the door.

Kerri tips her head to one side. "Would you really take his key if I asked you to?"

"I will do almost anything you ask me to do."

"What won't you do?"

I step toward her and pull her body against mine.

"Leave."

8

Kerri

I SLIP OUT from between the covers of my bed and pad across the floor to the bathroom. I move silently in the still dark room trying to channel my inner ninja.

"Good morning." Tracker rolls to his back on the bed. "You lose again."

I flip on the light.

His arm falls over his eyes. "Don't get mad about it." He squints at me under the shadow of his limb. "Wouldn't you be upset if I didn't hear someone sneaking around your bedroom?"

I flip the light back off. "Fine."

I'm a little crabby.

More than a little actually.

Considering how we started off, I never imagined I'd be here. With this extremely attractive man in my bed who's already had his hands all over me.

And in me.

Only he's using a completely different set of covers and sleeping in his clothes. With a pillow shoved between us.

And I thought I was frustrated before.

I walk into the bathroom and start the shower. At least I get to go to work today. It will be a much needed distraction and might make me feel like I still have the same life as before. That I'm still the same me as before.

Even if it's not true.

By the time I finish my shower and come out of the bathroom in my robe Tracker is up and moving with coffee and breakfast made. He hands me a cup and my eyes linger over the dark images inked into the skin of his arm. I take the cup. He pulls back and runs his hand down the arm I'm fascinated by.

"What do they mean?" I pull out a chair and sit down at the table.

Tracker sets a bowl of oatmeal on the table in front of me. "What does what mean?"

He understood the question. I know he did. "The tattoos on your arm."

Tracker turns and leans against the tiny bit of counter in the small kitchen of my apartment. He crosses his arms so the clear arm covers the one I'm asking about. He stares past me for a second before his eyes drop to the ground between us. "I was an angry kid."

I sip at my coffee, forcing myself to wait for him to continue.

"I was in foster care from the time I was ten." Evan glances at me for a second and I feel like he's waiting for me to react. So I don't.

"My parents were drug addicts who basically left me to fend for myself." He shoots me the look again.

I still don't react.

"I did whatever it took to survive. I stole. I fought. I hid." His eyes have a faraway look in them as he continues. "Some of the foster homes were worse than where I came from so I would run away and live on the streets, staying one step ahead of whoever was looking for me."

My stomach drops. That's how he became what he is now. Tracker learned to find people by first learning how to hide from them. I feel sick to my stomach as I imagine a small little boy sleeping in the cold. Alone.

Completely alone.

I can't cry. If I do he will never tell me anything again.

Because Evan means it when he says he will protect me.

So I sit there like my heart isn't breaking for him. Like it's not taking every ounce of strength in me to keep from melting into a puddle of tears. I stir the oatmeal he gave me, trying to focus on the bits of dried fruit and nuts he added. I should stay in my seat and force myself to act like what he said is no big deal. Then maybe someday he will tell me more.

But I can't.

Because all I want to do right now is hold the broken little boy who managed to somehow become a decent man. More than decent.

I stand up and go to him because I have to. I rest my hands on either side of his face. He won't look at me and that's okay. I understand. And I need him to know that.

So I kiss him. Because I need to feel better and I want him to feel better. Not that I'm self-centered enough to believe a kiss from me will wash away all the pain he's had to endure. But it might help right now in this minute. We can deal with the next minute when we get there.

His lips are so soft. Especially compared to the rasp of stubble covering his chin as it rubs against my skin. I don't care. It's the perfect combination. Rough and soft. Like him.

I hook one hand around his neck and shove the other into the wave of his sandy hair, pushing the tips of my fingers along his scalp. I want to taste him. I lick along the seam of his lips.

Without warning, Evan grabs me tight around the waist and switches our places, lifting me off the ground and setting my bottom on the counter. I wrap my legs around his waist and pull him tight against me as his mouth crushes against mine. This time he's the one kissing me. Hard. Rough. Needy.

The towel twisted around my hair topples to the floor. His hand grabs my damp locks, fisting them tight. He uses the grip to pull my head back so his mouth can move to my neck, licking and biting my skin. He moves to my ear. Sucking my lobe between his teeth.

"You're so perfect." His voice is a low growl against my skin. He pulls the neck of my robe over my shoulder and tastes his way down my throat and across my collarbone before pulling away.

He's stopping again. Putting the brakes on something I want more than I should.

I try to grab at him. Keep his body close to mine but he catches my wrist and holds it. He shakes his head at me. "You can control everything else, Kerri. Not this."

He pulls my hand to one side while his fingers work the knot at my waist, freeing it in a few seconds. Evan drops my wrist and uses both hands to spread my robe. His eyes roam my naked body, the fingers from one hand trailing his gaze, burning a path of fire with his touch. His other hand hooks under my knee from the inside and lifts my leg out and away from my body, opening my pussy to his gaze. His hand runs down my center, between my breasts and over the curve of my belly. "Beautiful."

I can't breathe, waiting to see what he will do next. I'll take whatever he wants to give me and probably still hope for more. I've never been with someone like Evan before and I can't get enough of the way he makes me feel. Strong but submissive. In control but under control.

And sexy. Really, really sexy.

I am suddenly concerned I may have bitten off more than I can chew with this man. He doesn't give me much time to entertain the thought because a second later his mouth is on me and I forget everything except the way he makes me feel.

Powerful.

Protected.

Desired.

His mouth is hot and wet as he laps at my clit, sucking it gently between his teeth until my thighs lock around his neck.

Holy shit, not again.

"Evan I—" It's too late. I grab his hair and hold his mouth against me as I come for him for the second time.

In under thirty seconds.

My head falls back against the cabinet as he stands between my legs and pulls me into his arms.

"You don't give me much time to enjoy myself." I hear the smile in his voice as he nuzzles my neck.

"Don't get cocky." I push at him. "You've seen what I'm used to."

His body tenses. "Have I?"

It's a simple question that I immediately regret giving him the opportunity to ask. Tracker is not going to like finding out the man he considers a pussy has been in mine.

Oh shit. That reminds me. I shove him for real this time and jump off the counter grabbing my robe as I go. "What time is it?"

Tracker leans against the counter, his eyes narrow. "Please don't tell me you fucked that guy from your work."

I pull my robe on as I rush to my room. "I won't."

I check the clock on my nightstand and feel a little better. I pull out a skirt and shirt and hurry to my dresser to snag panties and a bra. I manage to get on everything but my skirt by the time he makes it to the doorway.

"So what you're telling me is that guy fucked you and still ran away when a dangerous man grabbed you in a parking lot?" Tracker's voice is even and deep. Each word carefully enunciated and spaced perfectly against the next.

I have my skirt in my hands and pause to look up at him. "You're not dangerous."

"That's not true, Kerri." Tracker watches me closely. "Under the right circumstances I am capable of things you wouldn't imagine."

I zip up my skirt. "You can't kill Nelson."

"Yes. I can."

I tip my head back and blow out a breath. Jesus. One minute I'm embarrassing myself on a counter and the next I'm arguing against homicide. "Okay. I will concede that you are possibly capable of killing him." I look back at him with my eyebrows raised, giving him my serious teacher face. "What I'm saying is just because you can, doesn't mean you should."

He works his jaw from side to side.

I roll my eyes and push around him. I don't have time to watch him mull this over. "And he would probably die of heart failure if you even got too close to him." I turn around and push past him again back into my room. I grab my forgotten shoes from the closet and hold them up in explanation as I pass again.

I stop by the bathroom to pull my hair back into a bun and grab my tube of mascara. Tracker leans against the doorway as I fight a brush through my hair.

"So you're saying I could accidentally kill him and that would be acceptable?"

I flip off the bathroom light and push him toward the door. "No killing." I grab my work bag off the table as we pass and pause at the door to slip my shoes on. Tracker stuffs his feet into his boots and grabs the car keys off the entry table.

"You're no fun, Numbers."

****

"You're sure I can't kill him?" Tracker glares down the hall as Nelson stands outside his office chatting way too comfortably with a student.

"I'm positive." I open the door to my classroom and flip on the lights. "Are you sure you don't want to stay in my office?" I turn and find Evan still outside the door staring at Nelson and the girl who can't be more than nineteen. He finally turns to look at me. I smile. "There's free wifi."

Evan walks into the room slowly, his eyes moving around the space. "I want to stay close to you until we know exactly who wrote that message on your door."

I can't imagine they would risk grabbing me in the middle of a lecture but then again I would never imagine many of the things my father and people like him would do.

I look at the man wandering around my room like he's in a museum. How did he end up one of my father's members? Evan isn't the kind of man I remember from my childhood. Those men were older. Harder. Louder.

I wonder what the club's like now. Are most of the members like Evan...

Or my father?

I mentally shake myself. It doesn't matter what the club is like. That is not my life.

Never will be.

I take a deep breath and check the clock. "My students will be here soon." I point to a spot at the back of the room. "This is a smaller class so there will be plenty of empty seats." I grab a notebook off my desk and drop it in front of him along with a pencil. "If you just sit there it will be weird. I'm sure it won't be the most exciting hour you've ever spent but try to look like you're listening at least a little."

He opens the notebook. "You might be surprised at what I find exciting, Numbers."

I lean down and look him in the eye. "It's Ms. Wallace."

I straighten as the first of my class wanders through the door, barely giving Tracker a second look as they sit down and start to get organized for my lecture. This is my favorite class. It's a gen-ed algebra class so I get everyone. Students from all walks of life and all ages. People who haven't even thought of math in years.

I love it. I love the challenge of proving math isn't as scary as they think it will be. That they are capable of more than they could imagine.

I start my lecture, purposely ignoring the man sitting near the back beside Carlos because for some reason it makes me a little nervous to have him there, watching me do something I'm proud of. Something I worked very hard to achieve. It's probably about as exciting as dirt to him and I shouldn't be worried he's quietly judging me for loving math. I take a deep breath and try to relax.

After a few minutes I forget he's there, which is actually a mistake because then I accidentally look Evan's way. What I see scatters my train of though and leaves me speechless.

He's helping Carlos.

Evan points to the work I have neatly laid out across the board and then back to the notebook in front of him. His voice is low enough I can't hear what he's saying but it's clear who's doing the explaining.

My heart skips a beat.

I am so screwed.

9

Tracker

THE RIDE HOME is a little too quiet. Actually, Kerri has been quiet since her classes for the day ended. Maybe she's just all talked out but I don't think that's it. It's something else that's bothering her.

"I'm not trying to be invasive." I glance at her. She doesn't even look my way so I keep going. "I just don't want to assume you're going to be safe at work. It's not worth the risk."

Her head snaps to face me. "So, you're smart."

It's not a question. It's a statement of fact but it sounds more like an accusation and I don't know how to take it, so I shrug.

Her eyes zero in on the side of my face. "Why in the hell are you working for my father if you're smart?"

I know she doesn't mean it as in insult and I don't take it as one. It's actually a question I've been asking myself a lot lately. One I haven't found a good answer to yet. I know how I started with the club but as far as why I'm still there? "It's not something you can just quit doing, Kerri. You know that."

"Do you want to quit?" The words rush out of her mouth.

I pull into her parking space beside Butch's bright yellow Camaro. "It doesn't matter what I want."

I owe her father my life. He's made that very clear to me on any occasion I stepped too close to being out of line. I'm sure King will mention the debt again when he deals with what happened at his house. And he *will* deal with it.

Kerri's father rules the club with an iron fist. It's how our small little independent club managed to eat up more and more territory over the past ten years. Taking out anyone and everyone in our way. Doing whatever her father told us.

Because we had to.

As a kid I didn't realize what King was doing when he took me in. Even if I did, at eighteen I wouldn't have cared. It would have been worth it. For the first time I was fed and clothed and had a warm bed to sleep in.

So I did whatever he asked of me.

King said steal. I asked how much.

King said find them. I asked how fast.

King said burn it down. I asked how hot.

But now I'm not so sure I want to do what he asks. I'm not so sure I agree with the way he's built his empire.

Actually, I am sure.

I don't want to do anything he asks and I don't agree with anything he does. Including the way he treats his daughter and wife.

Especially the way he treats them.

I climb out of Kerri's car and open her door. She slides her hand into mine and climbs out, giving Butch a little wave as we walk to her apartment. "What about Butch?"

Butch is my best friend in the world. Has been for five years now. I don't know as much about his past and he doesn't know too much about mine but I would guess we're more alike than I know.

And we're a lot alike.

"He struggles like I do." I open the door to her apartment and let her go in. "I'll be in in a minute." I pull the door shut and go to find out if anything interesting happened today.

I know nothing happened here. Butch would have called me, but there's something else I've been keeping my eye on and I want to know if my friend has heard anything on that front.

He rolls down his window as I approach. Butch tips his head back in greeting. "Sup."

I lean down, resting my palm on the top of his car. "Anything?"

Butch shakes his head. "Nope. Not a thing. Pecker hasn't left his house today at all."

I look around the quiet parking lot. "I guess we just keep an eye on him and make sure he's not up to something behind our backs."

Butch frowns at me. "He's always up to something behind our backs."

King is always playing a game. And we were his pawns. Just like every other kid he recruited to be a part of his 'organization'. The man who was once the closest thing I ever had to a father is different than I thought. Or maybe it's me that's different.

I used to look up to Kerri's dad in a fucked up sort of way. He got what he wanted, when he wanted it. It didn't matter what it took or how many people he had to take down in the process. He was ruthless. He was callous.

He was crazy.

I can see that now.

And King's only getting crazier. That's why we started to watch him.

I glance at Kerri's door to make sure it's still shut. "He tried to knife anyone else at the clubhouse?"

"No." Butch rubs his hands down his face. "This is the craziest thing I've ever seen."

I straighten. "We just all have to stick together until we figure out what's got him wound up."

In the ten years I've been in the club I've never seen the president like he is now and I'm worried. In the weeks before I came to protect Kerri he was increasingly paranoid and hostile. It was a double-edged sword being assigned to a job so far away. It meant I was away from him but it also meant I wasn't there to help protect the newer members. The young kids he recruited over the past few years who still feel like I used to. They're the ones most at risk because they won't expect it when he turns on them.

Just like the one he tried to stab a few days ago.

Butch slides his window back up as I walk away, the weight of what's happening in the club resting heavy on my shoulders. I know he feels the same way. I can see it in his face. It helps to know I'm not alone. I'm not the only one who's realizing what King's doing is fucked up. That the way our club is run isn't the way other clubs are run.

I give my friend a wave before I close the door and lock the deadbolt. I take a deep breath and stare at it, trying to get my head on right for Kerri.

"What's wrong?"

I put on my game face and turn around. "Nothing." I take in the change in her appearance. Flannel shorts and an oversized v-neck t-shirt. "Not planning on going anywhere I take it?"

She wrinkles her nose at me. "Ha ha." Kerri flops down on the couch. She eyes my dark wash jeans and fitted t-shirt. "What does a man like you wear to relax?"

I give her a smile. "Nothing."

She raises an eyebrow. "In that case, yes I plan on staying in tonight." Kerri rests one bare foot on the coffee table and crosses the other over it. "Relaxing." She folds her hands in her lap and stares at me.

It's a challenge.

One she doesn't expect me to take.

Lucky her I'm feeling particularly generous this evening.

I peel my shirt off over my head.

Kerri straightens and her eyes widen. Other than that, she doesn't move. I'm pretty sure she's not even breathing at this point. Her eyes are on my chest, moving slowly over the images my skin has collected over the years. It's like a timeline of my life. Of my pain. Hopefully one day, of my happiness.

I stop as the last bit registers.

I've never let myself consider finding happiness. It was another thing I knew wasn't meant for men like me. Men who've done bad things. Men who've hurt people. Men who are so broken there's nothing strong enough to fix them.

But then I found something that might be strong enough.

I toe off my boots and kick them in front of the door. My fingers work the button on my jeans as I watch her. No one's ever looked at me like she does. Like I'm more than nothing.

I push down the zipper and let my pants drop to the floor.

Kerri sucks in a breath. I'm not sure if it's because I don't wear anything under my jeans or if it's the fact that a permanent reflection of my life is etched all the way down the left side of my body, inked over my ribs, down my hip and onto one thigh. I step out of my pants, pushing my socks off with them and straighten.

I watch her throat work as she swallows. I feel naked under her gaze, but not because I'm bare.

Because she sees me. Not Tracker. Not the outlaw biker I had to be to survive. Not one of her father's men.

Kerri sees *me*.

And it scares the shit out of me.

She sits silent on the couch as my stomach ties itself in knots. Today she saw one side of me. The side of me that could have been so much more if only things were different. But she needs to see this side of me too. I won't let her pretend it's not there. I can't.

Because it will always be a part of me, no matter what else happens in my life I will always be the little boy no one wanted. The little boy who went hungry for days. The little boy who didn't have shoes that fit until I was a grown man.

When Kerri's eyes meet mine my heart stops.

She blinks quickly, shoving back the shimmer of tears edging her lids. "Evan, you're beautiful."

I've been called many things in my life by women. Hot. Sexy. Asshole.

Never beautiful.

Not until her.

I shouldn't touch her when I feel like this. Raw. Vulnerable. Exposed.

It will make me think this is more than it is. Maybe I already do.

"Come here."

Kerri stands slowly. Her feet don't make a sound as she moves across the floor toward me. Her hands reach me before she does, gently brushing across the kaleidoscope of my past, skating over my skin with a feathery soft touch the images etched in pain don't deserve. A gentleness that belies the anger that created them. Then she steps closer.

Now it's her lips that trace the map of my past, moving slow across my shoulder, kissing down my arm and over my chest, brushing across my hip as she drops to her knees in front of me. I know what she's thinking and any other time I'd be thinking the same thing. Just not now.

I lean down and scoop her up. She's easy to hold and will be hard to let go, harder after today.

Maybe even impossible.

I carry her down the hall to her room. I lay her across the bed and ease over her, letting my body rest against hers as I cover her mouth with mine. I love how she tastes. Warm and sweet. Like her.

I lick inside her mouth, rubbing my tongue against hers. I leave her lips to kiss across her cheek and along her jaw. I breathe in her scent, letting the fresh smell of spring burn into my memory. It reminds me of sunshine and new beginnings. Maybe that's what this is for me.

A new beginning.

But that would mean I had a beginning to start with.

"Evan I—" She works her legs under my body until they clear my hips. Then she curls them at my sides.

My dick rests tight against her. Right where I want to be. Where I will be.

I push up her shirt, bunching the soft fabric under her arms until her full breasts are displayed to me. I lean up on one elbow and take in the beauty of the perfect view that is mine alone. I cup my hand around the soft curve of one and push it up to meet my lips. Her nipple is hard before I even touch it, puckering under my tongue and tightening even more as I suck it deep into my mouth.

Kerri's hands fist in my hair as she writhes under me. I take my time enjoying the most perfect body I've ever seen, let alone touched. I love how it feels under mine. Soft. Welcoming. Feminine.

I love the gentle curve of her stomach and the fullness of her hips and I show her. With my hands. With my mouth.

I want to taste her again. Feel the swell of her clit as I eat her until she screams. But that will have to wait.

Because this time I want her to come on me.

With me.

I lean up and drag her shorts down her long, strong legs, letting my hands rake over the contour of her thighs. I don't dare touch her anywhere else. Not until I get what I want from her.

What I need.

Then I remember. What I need is in my pants.

By the front door.

A perfect moment stalled. Shit.

I lean down and kiss her again, hoping it will be enough to smooth over the awkward moment I'm about to create. I hover over her. "I'll be right back."

Kerri reaches her hand behind her head, under the pillow she sleeps on. She pulls out a square foil pack and holds it in the air between us. "Do you still have to go?"

I pluck it from her fingers. "No. No I don't." I pull her shirt the rest of the way off. I want to feel all of her under all of me. It takes longer than it should to tear open the wrapper and roll the condom on. My hands are shaking like it's my first time.

It is.

The first time I've been with anyone I cared about. The first time sex was more than a way to get off and to feel like I was wanted by someone, even if it was only for one thing.

This is different for more reasons than I can count.

I look down at Kerri as I ease between her thighs. "Are you sure you want to do this?"

I have to give her an out because I don't know that I am strong enough to give her one after this.

She reaches up and cups my face with both hands. "I'm more than sure."

I don't wait. I can't. Not one second longer to have her. I watch her face as I push inside the heat of her body. I groan as her walls tighten around me, sucking me deeper into her pussy. Her head falls back and her eyes shut as my body fills hers, sinking in until there is no more of me to give.

"Oh my God." Her lips barely move as the whisper slips through them. "Evan."

Any control I believe I have over the situation evaporates when she says my name. I lace my fingers through her hair as I start to move, impaling her body with mine, holding her tight. I need to know she's real. That this is happening.

To me.

I lift my eyes to the mirrors on her closet and watch us. Watch her fingers digging into my skin, marking me, digging new lines beside the old. Changing the landscape of my life with a swipe of her hand. Her legs lock around my waist, holding me as tightly as I hold her.

"Evan I—" I know it's all the warning I'm going to get. Luckily it's all I need.

"Come for me." I tuck my head against her neck, breathing her in as I fill her with long, strong strokes. I feel my dick twitch inside her, ready. I dig deep and hold on a little longer, waiting for what I have to have. My vision narrows and any other thoughts scatter as I try to focus on making sure I come with her.

"Oh God." Her thighs clench against my waist as her pussy starts to spasm around my cock.

"Kerri, please." My cock swells and my balls pull up tight as I come, shuddering as her walls milk the pleasure from my body with her own.

I fight to catch my breath as I collapse onto her. It's only a few seconds before I realize I'm probably suffocating her. She holds me tight as I start to roll off her.

"Stay here just a minute longer." Her hands trail up my back, smoothing over the scratches I know I will hate to see fade.

I lean up just enough to brush my lips over hers. "I'll stay as long as you want."

She smiles. "I'll remember you said that."

10

Kerri

I SIT UP straight in bed and reach beside me. I don't know what dragged me out of the deepest sleep I've had in a long time but I know what's keeping me from falling back into it.

My bed's empty.

But my apartment's not so that's some consolation.

I can hear the low rumble of Evan's voice in my living room and it pulls me from my bed to go find him. I creep across the floor and stand in the doorway, holding my breath so I can hear what he says.

"If you come near King's daughter you will have worse things to worry about then her daddy coming after you." Evan's voice is a lethal sounding hiss. "He won't get the chance."

I press one hand to my mouth and the other to my rolling stomach as he keeps talking to whoever is on the other end of his phone.

"I will hurt you in ways you can't imagine." The ice in his tone carries through the apartment and runs down my spine.

It's not Evan on the phone. It's Tracker.

The apartment goes silent. I peek around the wall.

He's standing in the middle of my living room. His back is to me and I can see the tension across his shoulders, even in the dim light filtering through the blinds.

He turns abruptly and I don't have time to retreat if I wanted to.

"How long have you been awake?" His words are cautious, hesitant.

"Long enough to know there's a problem." I swallow down the panic rising in my throat and force myself to stay calm. "What did they say?"

Tracker shakes his head. "Nothing."

"I need to know what's going on." I walk toward him. "Please don't keep me in the dark thinking you're protecting me from something I already know." I rest my forehead against the warm skin of his chest. "I lived in that world until I was eighteen. I know what goes on."

Evan's arms wrap around my back. "I'm not sure you know as much as you think you do, Kerri."

His phone starts to ring. The glow of the screen illuminates the space around us. His whole body goes rigid when he looks at the screen. Tracker sucks a breath in through his nose and swipes his thumb across the screen connecting the call. "Yeah."

"Yeah?" The silence of night and the closeness of our bodies makes it easy for me to hear the other end of the conversation. The voice

breath then reaches for me, pulling me tight against his chest. So tight it almost hurts. And I like it.

I wrap my arms around him and close my eyes, focusing on the slow, steady beat of his heart under my ear. "Please tell me what's happening."

He rests one cheek against the top of my head. "I can't."

"Can't or won't?"

"Both." Evan reaches up to cup my face with both hands. He tips my head back. His eyes are intense as they search mine. "All I want is to keep you safe and I will do whatever it takes to make that happen."

"Including keeping things from me?"

He doesn't hesitate. "Yes."

I tense up at his admission. The confirmation doesn't sit well. I know what can happen when a woman lets someone else make decisions for her. I've seen it first hand and I won't be that woman. Not for anyone.

His hands press into my face. "Don't be upset."

"I will do whatever I want." I pull my face free of his hold and back away. "I thought you understood."

"I do." Tracker stays put. "I understand more than you think and I know it's hard but I need you to trust me right now. Trust that I will keep you safe and when it's all over I will tell you everything I know." His lips quirk up at the sides. "And then you can boss me around all you want."

I cross my arms over my chest and stare at him. He's not mad. He didn't yell. He didn't raise a hand to me, thank God, because I didn't take self-defense classes for nothing. He's actually just standing there almost smiling at me.

"All I want?"

Now he's definitely smiling. "All you want."

I narrow my eyes at him. "You'll do whatever I say?"

"Anything."

I run my tongue over my teeth as I consider it. I don't like not knowing what's happening but...

I kind of sort of trust him. A little.

"Okay." It isn't quite as painfully terrifying as I expected to give him this. It's awful feeling, but on another level it's also a little freeing to let go of a small bit of the untrusting part of me created by my past.

His shoulders drop the smallest bit. "Thank you."

I point at him. "Don't get used to it."

Because I won't. I can't. I won't be my mother and if I think for a second that's where this is headed Tracker will be out on his ass.

"I wouldn't think of it." He holds one hand out to me. "Come here."

I shake my head. "You come here."

"And so it begins." He flashes me a grin then out of nowhere he rushes me, bending at the waist and resting his shoulder on my middle before standing up, taking my flailing body with him. "You are a hellion, Kerosene Danger. I love it."

****

"I don't like that guy." I stare through the front window of my apartment at the giant of a man standing next to Butch's lemon yellow sports car.

Tracker looks at me. He tips his head down and lowers his voice. "Why?"

I shake my head. "I don't know."

"I need more than an I don't know." Tracker looks out at the man with Butch and then back at me. "Can you give me any specific reason?"

'Because he looks scary' probably doesn't count as more than I don't know. I glance at the man beside me. Plus I would guess Tracker might be a notch higher on the scaryometer to some people. The man outside my apartment doesn't have a single tattoo that I can see but I know he has to at least have one. The Knight's club mark is somewhere on his body.

He's tall. Like, really tall. Crazy tall. And wide. Like a bus. Other than that I've got no reason other than a sixth sense to explain why he makes me feel...

Cautious.

I shake my head. "Just a feeling."

Tracker nods. "I'll keep that in mind."

I slide my eyes Tracker's way and study him. His statement didn't sound condescending or even a little sarcastic. Like he was really going to take my odd feeling into account.

"You still have to deal with him." Tracker grabs my keys and opens the door. "Your father thinks you need another set of eyes on you and Hawk's are the ones he picked."

I wrinkle my nose. "Hawk?"

Tracker shrugs. "I didn't pick it."

I look out at the man who looks more like a Tank or maybe a tongue-in-cheek Tiny. "Who did?"

"Your dad. He chooses all the road names." Tracker holds his hand out for me to head outside.

My dad picks the names? That's not how it used to work. I remember the men who hung around my house as a kid. There was no story they loved to tell more than the one about how they got their road names. "That's strange."

Tracker looked at me, his brow lined in confusion. "Why do you say that?"

"What in the hell is going on out here today?" Violet steps outside her door and glares at me and my rapidly growing entourage. "You are the loudest group of boys I've ever met in my damn life."

I stop and stare at her. I've never seen my neighbor in anything other than a housecoat, so the sight of her in a floral polyester pants suit throws me off. "Are you going somewhere, Violet?"

Her head turns my way. Finally her eyes join it. "What? Oh." She looks down at the button-up jacket, smoothing her bony hand down the front. "Well. You never know." She winks at Evan. "Maybe I'll steal one of your men and make him take me to dinner." She looks from Butch to Hawk to Tracker. "You've got more than your share."

I let out a long sigh. "Don't I know it." I walk toward my car. Evan rests one hand on the small of my back and leans in close.

"Butch is taking you to work today." He glances at Hawk. "I'm going to hang back here with Hawk and keep an eye on things."

I look at Butch then back at Tracker. "I don't want to do that."

He leans down and presses a chaste kiss against my lips. "I need you to." He pulls me against his chest and tucks his head into my neck so no one will hear what he says. "Remember you will get to be the boss as soon as this is all over." He sucks my earlobe between his teeth. "Not in the bedroom though."

I shake my head. "You already made the deal. No amending it now." I push at him, wriggling free of his hold. I stand in front of the Tweety Bird toned car that's been sitting in front of my apartment like a giant arrow for the past week. Hell it's no wonder they found me. I point at Butch then motion to the car. "Come on then."

Tracker opens my door as Butch climbs in the driver's side. Evan leans in and gives me another kiss. I expect him to tell me to be careful. He doesn't.

"Be nice."

I smile at him. "I'm always nice."

"Shit." He looks across the car at Butch. "Don't let her scare you."

His friend starts the car and the engine revs to life. "Too late." Butch gives me a wink.

I roll my eyes. Now I have to be nice to him because he's funny.

Tracker closes the door and steps back. Butch pulls out of the parking space next to mine and I watch Tracker in the side mirror as we pull out of the lot. He stands tall next to Hawk even though he's a few inches shorter than the bigger man. We turn down the drive that skirts the side of my building and he's gone from sight.

I stare out the windshield. Not having Tracker at my side makes me feel different about everything that's going on and it makes me realize something.

I trusted him longer than I knew I did. For no good reason either.

Almost from the start I knew Evan meant it when he said he would protect me. As a result I haven't been diligent myself, believing he would take care of me. But now I feel different. Is it because he's not at my side for the first time in over a week? Or is it something else?

The same something I couldn't pinpoint earlier.

"You and Tracker seem to be getting along well." Butch's voice is deep and gravely. Rough. Not unpleasant, just not the smooth timbre I'm used to hearing from Evan.

"Uh-huh." Why do I feel suspicious of him all the sudden? Without Tracker to tell me how to feel I'm questioning everyone and everything.

Except him.

And he trusts Butch.

Enough to let me ride off with him alone.

Which is great but I'm going to reserve judgment until I get to work in one piece.

Butch slows to a stop at a red light and turns to me. "Tracker isn't like most of the people living this life."

"That's good to know." I watch Butch closely, trying to get a read on him since I haven't worried as much as I should about him. I study his clothes. The watch on his wrist. The single tattoo on his arm.

He shifts in his seat and looks away.

Interesting.

I know Tracker said to trust him. That he would take care of me and I believe he will do everything he can.

I also believe I'm not the kind of girl who blindly lets a man tell me what to do. Even though I somehow forgot that recently.

I'm not being defiant. I'm not going to revolt against the small bit of footing I've accidentally allowed Evan to have in my life. But it won't hurt a thing if I'm prepared to hold my own and that starts by paying better attention to what's happening around me instead of having my head in the sand. Or up my ass depending on how you look at things.

A few minutes later Butch pulls into the faculty lot at the university. I expect him to drop me off at the doors but instead he parks.

"What are you doing?" I point to the glass entry. "You can just drop me off."

Butch shakes his head. "Nope. I don't want to die today." He pulls a leather bag from the back seat and climbs out. I open my door and push up from the low vehicle, smoothing the back of my skirt as I shut the door. I start across the parking lot toward the doors, not looking to see if Butch is following me.

"Kerri."

Ugh. My brain can't handle this today.

Nelson slow jogs toward me in his plaid suit coat and tie. "I'm glad I caught you." He looks around quickly. "I wanted to make sure everything's okay."

"You mean you wanted to make sure the man you were going to let abduct me didn't murder me." I keep walking, tugging my work bag higher on my shoulder.

"Well, I mean, I knew he didn't murder you. I saw you at work the next day." Nelson's feet skip as he tries to keep pace with me. "I saw those men that were looking for you and I wanted to be sure you weren't in some kind of trouble."

I stop and turn to face him. "What men?"

He looks taken aback. "Well the men that looked like that other guy." He leans in. "Like criminals."

I glance around the parking lot, making a slow sweep with my eyes. Butch is a decent clip away near the doors sitting on a bench. Well out of earshot. "Where did you see them?"

"Here. I mean inside. Around your office." Nelson's face goes white. "Oh my God." He steeples his hands over his mouth. "*Are* they criminals?"

That's the problem I'm currently having myself.

I wanted to forget they are criminals. To pretend my old life wasn't sucking me back in and pulling me under to drown in the same past I fought to escape.

I look Nelson in the face and lie to him. "Nope." I force a smile. "Thank you for your concern though."

I spin on my heel and walk to the doors, ignoring Butch as he eases off the bench and follows me inside. I unlock my office and immediately open the door to my classroom and flip on the lights. I point into the room. "Should I assume you're planning on sitting in on my classes today?"

"I go where you go." Butch wanders into the classroom and sits as far back as he can, dropping his bag on the table and fishing out a book. He leans back and flips it open to the bookmarked spot and starts reading.

These fucking bikers are not at all what I remember.

And I'm not sure that's a good thing.

11

Tracker

I STARE UP at the first home I ever had. I've only been away from the large two-story building for two weeks but it feels like forever. I may not live there anymore but it was still an important part of my life. It's the home base for all the club's activities since a high number of the members still live there. It's where we gather. Where we meet up before riding. Where we are given orders.

And it's where we were all first brought when Kerri's dad recruited us. Where we learned to be brothers.

"How many are here?" I look over at Butch. He's staring up at the house the same way I am. He's one of the few current members who was over twenty when he joined. He's also one of the few who sought the club out.

He counts the motorcycles lined under a long carport. "At least fifteen."

Most of the younger members still only have a bike to get around. It's the first thing Kerri's dad does now when he's trying to convince a kid to join. He buys them a bike. It's usually the first time anyone's ever given them anything. It's the beginning of the debt he reminds you is yours. It's how he controls you. It's how he has gotten as far as he has.

The guilt of lost boys who just want someplace to belong.

"Do we have any idea where they stand?" The balance in the club is shifting like quicksand. The men who came in around the time I did are older and wiser then when the head of a bike club was able to woo their loyalty with a motorcycle and a warm bed. There are at least ten of us. Ten men questioning everything we thought we knew about King and The Knights.

And we're angry.

But we're not the only side to the story. Some of my brothers don't see things the way we do. They still want to believe what Kerri's dad does is right instead of seeing the truth in what King does.

Butch presses his lips into a thin line and shakes his head. "That's the million dollar question, my friend."

We have to be careful. Between the turf war King's never-ending greed started and the tension among the brothers, there's a real chance someone could get hurt tonight. But we can't wait. Something has to be done before King can launch us into an all-out war, either with another club or with each other.

"Let's take it real easy then." I start up the sidewalk to the plain cement building hidden in an industrial area at the edge of town. It looks like a warehouse, and it is. Just not for supplies of the normal type.

This is where King keeps his human supplies.

The kids he woos from the streets, from poverty, from juvie, from boys homes. He gives them things they never dreamed of. Showering them with praise and attention.

But the devil always calls in his favors. And this demon keeps calling.

Butch opens the door and I step through it into the smoky air of the main living area. It was the part I hated about living here, even from the beginning. The stale stink of King's habit permeates everything in the building. Just like the darkness I know is inside him.

"What in the hell are you two motherfuckers doing here?" Kerri's dad sits in his recliner, a cigarette dangling from his mouth and a beer resting on his leg. He snarls in my direction. "Where is my fuckin' daughter?"

See, that's the part of this that doesn't make sense to me. I didn't even know King had a daughter. Not until I was ordered to leave my post as a sort of private investigator for the club and go an hour away to protect her. Why is he suddenly so worried about Kerri's safety? Is it some sort of twisted sense of honor?

No. It isn't.

That's not the kind of man King is. He honors one person and one person only.

Himself.

"She's with Hawk." I walk across the room, feigning an ease I don't feel in my old home. "I figured you'd be okay with it since you sent him." I sit down on the couch between two of the newer members of the club, an eighteen-year-old King found in a drug house and a twenty-year-old the old man bailed out of an assault charge. He brought them both here and took them under his wing, just like he did all of us.

I lean back against the sofa and spread my arms across the back. "I was missing this place. Wanted to stop by and visit."

King eyes me from his throne, gulping down a swallow of his beer. "In that case I'm glad to see you boys."

Boys. That's what he calls us. His boys. Now I realize it's another small way he maintains control of a group of men used to fighting for everything they have. He instills a sense of belonging and brotherhood none of us has had before.

It's careful. It's calculated. It's by design.

"Have you heard anything else from The Horsemen?" I keep my tone as casual as the situation warrants.

King looks around the group gathered in the living area. "No." He flips the lever on the side of his leather recliner and sits up. He holds his empty bottle out to one of the young men near him. "Take this in and get me another, son."

I swallow down my anger at what he's doing. What he's always done, as long as I've known him at least. That's around the time the older members of the club started leaving, ducking out for one reason or another, leaving King a skeleton of a club to preside over.

That's when he changed tactics.

He leans forward in his seat. "You fucking my daughter, Tracker?"

The question seems to come out of nowhere but I've known the old man too long to think it really does. I don't know what game he's playing and I don't want to play. Not when it comes to Kerri.

But I have to if I want to figure out how to save the club that saved me. It wasn't King that saved me the day he found me living on the street. It was the brothers I made. Like Butch.

I lift an eyebrow at his question as I debate my options. I can't say no. He won't believe it. I have to give him something he will believe.

"I tried." I shrug. "She wasn't having it."

King sneers out a snort. "Bitch doesn't know men are the ones who make the decisions."

I expected him to be pleased. No one wants to hear someone like me is fucking their daughter. I figured that even included him. But

King doesn't look happy to hear his daughter turned me down.

He looks pissed. He nods to Butch's position by the door. "What about you? You fuck her?"

Butch's eyes stay on King. "No, sir."

King drops his elbows to his knees and wipes one hand down his face, cupping the length of his beard as he drags it down the long wild gray mass. "So you're telling me neither of you boys has a thing for my daughter?"

Now Butch looks at me. Our eyes meet for a second before snapping back to King as he stands to pace. "Is that why you just left her with Hawk to come fuckin' hang out here? Because you don't really give a shit what happens to her?"

"Of course we care what happens to her." I keep my voice low and even, hoping it will keep him from launching over the edge he's been toeing for the past few months. I don't feel like getting knifed tonight and right now I would bet Butch and I are outnumbered by young guns who still feel a sense of loyalty toward the old

184

man for pulling them from their shit lives and tricking them into another shit life. One that isn't even their own.

It's his.

"She's your daughter King, and we want her to be safe. That's why I had you assign Butch to help me. That's why Hawk is there. We all want to protect her."

King stops pacing and stares at me. I don't flinch under the hard line of his gaze as he sizes me up. "Then I suppose I should thank you." He snaps his fingers and one of the younger men stands up from his seat. King's eyes don't leave me as he leans into the kid's ear and gives him an order loud enough for me to hear. "Go get Tracker one of the girls."

I don't fuck the misses. Never have. It's something King should know and that means one thing.

He's testing me.

And I'm going to fail.

"He doesn't have time for that shit." Butch pushes off the spot of wall he's been leaned against since we came in. "Hawk made us promise to be back before ten."

I hold my breath as Butch's lie hangs in the air. It was a big risk to take. Especially since we're not sure who's on our side and who's not.

"What's he got going on?" King snorted. "Maybe he's the one fucking my daughter." He stands tall and tips his head back before landing the blow that almost takes me down. "Maybe he wants to be sure you'll be back in time to watch."

It takes everything I have not to react. Not to punch the motherfucker in the face for what he's doing. For whatever game he's playing with all of us.

Now I see why The Horsemen are pushing back. Word's getting around that King is losing it. The clubs he's been systematically pushing out of their territories for the past ten years have been waiting for a chance like this.

I shrug. "As long as I don't have to touch his dick I'm game." I almost choke on the words but they come out clear and strong. As indifferent as I can make them.

Butch opens the door and nods for me to leave first, probably because he can tell how close I am to ruining everything. I take my time, swatting a couple of the newest recruits on the back as I leave. "See you boys later."

I suck fresh air into my lungs as I amble down the sidewalk, fishing my key from the pocket of my jeans. I run one hand through my hair as I resist the urge to run to my bike and break every law to get to Kerri's apartment and make sure she's okay. That I didn't just leave her with one of them.

I pull out my phone and dial her number. It goes to voicemail.

"What do you know about Hawk?" I don't look at Butch. I can't.

"I guess we'll find out." Butch swings one leg over his bike and looks at me. "Can she hold her own if—"

I hold up my hand, cutting him off as I snap my phone back in my jacket pocket. "Don't."

I can't think about what it could mean if Hawk is one of King's devotees. He's the generation of recruits stuck in the middle. Not the older jaded crowd I'm a part of and not the younger crowd that still lives in the house and idolizes King. I knew he could go either way. That's why I spent all day with the man and until a few minutes ago I was sure Hawk was on our side.

Now I'm not so sure.

My skin goes cold. What if this is about more than just The Horsemen? What if King is even more twisted than I know? At the time I thought part of the reason I was assigned to Kerri was because he was punishing me for the narrow line of insubordination I've been walking.

But what if he was hoping to punish her too?

Butch catches me across the chest with an outstretched arm as I turn to walk back into the clubhouse. "You can't." He puts pressure on me, pushing me back toward my bike. "The best thing we can do is get back to her and make sure everything's okay."

I kick my leg over my bike and fire it up. A hard ride home will take the edge off until I see her. Until I know I didn't just make a mistake that will cost us both.

Because I'll fucking go to jail tonight if Hawk's laid a finger on her.

****

"What in the fuck is going on here?"

Kerri looks up at me from her spot on the couch. "What?"

I point to the giant man passed out on the floor. Then I point to Shelly. "I mean how in the hell did these things happen?"

Kerri flashes me a smile. "I didn't drug him if that's what you're asking." Her tone is teasing but I'm not feeling amused.

Hawk stirs from his spot in the middle of the living room, lifting his head to look at me. "Oh, hey, Tracker." He smiles at me which is fucking weird because Hawk never smiles. At anyone. For any reason. "How'd it go?" He rolls to his back and yawns.

Butch walks through the door I left open and stops behind me. "What in the fuck is going on?"

"I'm trying to figure out the same thing." I look at Shelly. "How'd you get here?"

She pointed to Hawk. "He and Kerri came and picked me up."

"We're having a girl's night." Hawk grins at me from the floor. I didn't even know the bastard had teeth and now suddenly he's a barrel full of sunshine smiling like he doesn't have a care in the world.

I look at Kerri. "Please tell me you didn't give him that sparkle shit."

She stands up off the couch, her brown eyes flashing. "I told you I didn't drug him."

I point to the man lying on the floor staring at his hand. "I've known this guy for years and I've never seen him smile. Not one fucking time. And now he's—" I look down at Hawk who points a finger gun at me and clicks his tongue, giving me a wink. I rub my hand down my face. "He's fucking worthless." I walk across the floor without bothering to take off my boots. I've been worried sick about her for an hour and I come home to this. I grab her by the arm. "I can't believe you did this. Do you know how hard I'm working to make sure you're safe? Do you even care?"

The weight of keeping her safe, of keeping the club intact, of keeping King from pulling more unsuspecting kids into his web of manipulation and control, it's all barreling down on me and I'm not sure I can handle anymore. I grab her other arm, holding her in place. "Why can't you do a single thing I ask?"

Kerri leans back like I slapped her. She blinks at me, confusion clouding her eyes. "I can't believe you're saying this." Her voice is barely a whisper as she keeps blinking until her confusion clears, replaced by something that is a knee to my gut.

Hurt.

She pulls out of my hands and I let her go. She shakes her head at me. "I thought you were different. I thought you weren't like him. I—" Kerri presses her lips into a thin line. "Go." She points to Butch and Hawk. "Take them with you." She rushes into her bedroom and I hear the lock click on the door.

"You're a dick, Evan." Shelly stands up from the couch with her glass of wine. She points to the pile of biker on the floor at her feet. "For the record I'm the one who slipped Mr. Personality here a little sparkle in his punch this evening." She tips back a long swallow from her glass. "I figured it wouldn't hurt anything and he was being so damn serious."

Hawk points up at Shelly. "You're really pretty."

I could swear her skin pinks up just a little at the compliment. She opens her mouth to respond but Hawk cuts her off. He points at me.

"I think King knows you don't like him." He rolls around for a minute, struggling to sit up. Finally the big man manages to angle his upper half off the floor. "You wanna know a secret?" He waves me down close.

I look back at Kerri's closed bedroom door then I squat down next to Hawk. He rests his hand on my back and leans into my ear.

"I don't like him either."

12

Kerri

I STARE UP at the ceiling of my bedroom, blinking at the tears trying to fight their way out of my eyes. Damn things are acting like we cared about him or something.

The apartment has been quiet for a couple hours now. Shelly texted me an hour ago to let me know she made it to her apartment and that Butch was sitting outside her place in his ugly-ass yellow car because apparently he thinks now there is a chance she could be targeted too. Just for hanging out with me.

That was fucking great news.

I roll to my side trying to ease the pressure of a bladder full of wine pushing against my abdominal wall. It doesn't help. I throw off the covers and slide off my bed. I unlock my door and walk across the hall to the bathroom, do my business and then go to the kitchen to get a bottle of water. Between Shelly, Hawk and me we finished off three bottles of wine and I am going to have a hell of a headache tomorrow if I'm not careful.

I walk back toward my bedroom to go back to wallowing in my own stupidity. It's only then that I notice the shadow of a man on my couch. "Jesus fucking Christ." I throw my open water bottle square at where his face should be and rush back into the kitchen for a knife.

Why did I send everyone away? Now I had to kill someone on my own. I can't carry a body. Where would I even take a body to dump it?

A dumpster. That's where I'll take it. But only after I'm sure Violet's asleep and won't try to get in on the action. No witnesses. They're always the weak link.

The shadow jumps off my couch, sputtering. "Kerri, stop."

The knife is already clutched in my hand when the voice registers. I spin around. "I told you to leave."

Tracker comes toward me, wiping his face with one arm. "And I told you I would do anything you asked me to do except that."

I consider putting down the knife in my hand. I look down at it.

Nah.

Right now he deserves to think I would stab him. And he might not be as far off as I wish he was. I point the blade at him. "You are an asshole."

"Just stop." He keeps walking until the tip of my butcher knife almost touches his stomach. He's close enough I can smell him. The spicy richness comforts me which only pisses me off more.

He holds his hands up, palms facing me. "Please, just let me try to explain."

I shake my head. "I don't want to hear it." My grip on the knife handle tightens. "I won't live like my mother."

"Fuck."

The word is barely a whisper. One Tracker probably doesn't realize I heard. May not even realize he said. But he will. I nod my head at him. "Yeah. Fuck."

I still kinda want to stab him, just a little, not enough to damage anything important. But that wouldn't solve anything and it would get blood on the carpet I work really hard to keep clean. I set the knife on the counter. "And it's all for nothing because I really didn't drug your friend."

"I know." His head drops. "Shelly told me what happened."

I blink in the dark, wondering what Shelly had to explain. "I mean he drank a bunch of wine but he's a big dude so I didn't think it would be an issue. And it's not like we forced him."

Tracker's head lifts a little, his eyes slitted in confusion. "He didn't just have wine, Kerri."

No. Shelly wouldn't do that. I walk to the trash can and flip on the kitchen light. The tiny baggy of sparkle I tossed in earlier is still sitting where I put it.

Minus the sparkle.

My friend drugged Hawk. And she didn't even give me a heads up about it. "Is he okay?"

"Okay?" Tracker wipes at the droplets of water still clinging to his jaw line. Now that the lights are on and I can get a good look at him I realize something I didn't before.

He looks like total shit.

And it bothers me.

"He's probably going to be pissed as hell tomorrow but other than that he's fine." Tracker steps toward me.

I back up.

"Kerri, I'm sorry."

I wrap my arms around myself to keep from reaching for him. I don't feel good. My stomach is queasy, my head is already starting to throb, and my chest feels like someone is standing on it. I want him to make me feel better.

But he's the reason for two out of three of my problems.

"Why didn't you leave? I told you to leave." I wanted him to leave. I still think I want him to leave.

His head tips to one side as his eyes study my face. "It would take more than you telling me to leave to make me go."

I look up at him. "I also had a knife."

He shrugs. "I would've deserved it." His hand drifts to a spot on his chest.

My eyes are glued to the place his fingers are rubbing and the sick feeling I have in my stomach grows like a wildfire, burning through my belly and up my esophagus. "Have you been stabbed before?"

He ignores me. "I stayed because we need to talk." The hand over the spot I'm sure has felt the slide of a knife drops to his side. I want to push his shirt up and see for myself. Look at the place someone hurt him.

So I do.

I grab his t-shirt and shove it high on his chest until the spot I'm looking for is exposed. If I didn't know what I was looking for I would miss it. Hidden into a thin line on an image of the reaper is the raised pucker of a scar. I lift my hand and run one finger over it. I look over his skin, running my fingers across the dark images of death and destruction. I feel a patch of circular scars no bigger than the head of a pencil.

Or the lit end of a cigarette.

I swallow hard and let his shirt fall back into place.

I'm angry with him and the images in my mind of a little boy being hurt and abused shouldn't change that. He still screwed up. "I'm still mad at you." I say it out loud hoping to make it true.

"You should be." Evan's voice is soft and calm. "I fucked up, Kerri. Again." His hand starts to reach for me and then falls back to his side. "You don't have to forgive me but I'm not leaving you until all this is over and I know you're safe."

"How long will that be?" I try to imagine him going, leaving me. What would it be like to go back to the life I had before? The life I fought so hard to achieve. A life filled with smart, boring men with 401K's and college degrees who drove sensible cars and lived sensible lives. The kind of men I tried to force myself to be fulfilled by. Turned on by.

But I'm not.

"That's what we need to talk about." He steps back and I miss the smell of him. "Can we sit down though?"

I look over at the couch where Shelly, Hawk and I were laughing and drinking just a few hours ago without a care in the world. Especially Hawk. I close my eyes and cringe.

"I should have realized something was up when he started singing *Single Ladies.*"

Tracker lifts an eyebrow. "I'm going to need you to put a pin in that because I would be interested to hear that story." He rests his hand on the small of my back and directs me toward the couch. "Later."

It's the first time he's touched me since this morning and I missed the feel of part of him on part of me. I focus on the way his body heat soaks into my skin as I drag out the short walk to the sofa.

I'm still mad at him though.

I just like it when he touches me is all.

I sit down on the end cushion of the couch and tuck my legs under me. Tracker sits close beside me and I wonder if he feels like he's walking across a frozen pond right now. Trying to see how far he can get before falling through the ice and freezing to death.

"I'm still mad at you." I throw it out there not only to remind myself but also to keep him to the thicker parts of the ice for now. I don't want him to fall through and die.

That would be sad.

"I would hope so." He lays his arm across the back out the couch behind me. Not touching me, but still surrounding me in a way that makes me feel safe. Like I always do when he's there.

Even now.

Because never once has Evan been mad that I'm upset. Never once has he tried to convince me not to be mad about what he did. Never once has he made what happened my fault.

Which is bad because now I feel guilty for basically saying he is like my father. He's not. Evan is nothing like my father.

But I am.

My eyes burn and the tears I've been holding in spill over, running down my cheeks. Jerks. I don't have any extra hydration to spare right now.

"Kerri, I'm so sorry." He runs right to the middle of the metaphorical frozen pond and pulls me into his arms, risking life and limb to comfort me.

He doesn't die. He doesn't fall through. The ice doesn't even crack.

Because as much as I'm trying to be, I'm not still mad at him. Now I'm mad at myself.

I bury my head against his chest. "I'm sorry I said you were like my father."

He pulls me onto his lap and tucks my head under his chin. It feels so good to be in his arms again and for some reason that only makes me cry harder. Maybe I'm still drunk and that's what's making me emotional. Maybe I'm just tired.

Or maybe I just really, really like him and the idea of not having Evan in my life makes me a stupid, ugly-crying mess.

Yeah. That's the one.

His hand rubs up and down my back in long, slow lines. We sit like this for a minute, him quietly soothing me while I curl against him listening to the sound of his heartbeat.

He takes a breath.

"I was scared to death tonight, Kerri."

I lean back a little and look up at him. "Why?"

He pulls me back tight against him. "There are things going on in the club now that make it a dangerous group to be involved with."

Yeah. That's why he's here. "I know. My father's taking over territory and pissing everyone off."

Except me for once. I'm glad King did what he did. Not glad enough to stop wishing he was dead, but glad enough I don't still want to do it myself. If he hadn't, I would never have Evan.

And I think I might like to have him.

"How much do you know about how your father runs the club?" Evan's voice has an edge to it that wasn't there before.

"I know he took over when I was still in elementary school. I remember the other men coming over and hanging around in the garage at the back of our house. My dad was the club mechanic so they all brought their bikes for him to work on." It was always strange to me how kind the other bikers were to me and my mom, especially as I got older. It was a marked difference from how my father treated us. I wondered if those men were like my father behind closed doors. "As I finished high school, right before I left, there weren't as many men around."

"Do you know why?"

I shrug. "I didn't care enough to wonder. I was almost free. I couldn't wait to put all of them behind me."

Evan stiffens under me.

It's a topic I've been trying not to think about. I don't want to. I want to keep on going like we are. Me happily pretending Tracker isn't what he is.

"I can't leave the club, Kerri." His hand strokes down my hair. It's almost as soft as his voice in my ear saying words I didn't want to ever hear him say.

I'm not stupid, just trying to be in denial. I knew Evan couldn't leave The Knights. Not if my father had anything to say about it, and that pecker had something to say about everything.

Now I was back to wanting to kill King myself. For taking away one more thing that means something to me. First my mom.

Now Evan.

"But..."

My heart skips a beat. There's a but.

"I think there are some big changes coming." He slides the hand stroking my hair down to cup my cheek and tip my eyes up to meet his. "Can you still trust me?"

I chew on my bottom lip. I feel stupid admitting it easily, especially considering I wanted to stab him a little just a few minutes ago, so I drag it out, pretending it's not an easy decision. Like I wouldn't blindly follow him into a burning building if he told me to.

And I probably would.

Especially if he was naked.

Definitely if he was naked.

"I trust you."

The tension in his body eases a little at my admission. Evan leans in and brushes a kiss across my lips. "Why don't you go to bed and get some sleep."

I check the clock on the DVD player tucked beneath my television. It's 3am. Luckily my classes tomorrow are later in the day. Hopefully

I can sleep off the ache building behind my eyeballs from too much wine and too much crying and I'll feel better in the morning. But I'm not doing it alone.

"What about you?"

Tracker leans back. "I'll sleep out here."

"No."

"I fucked up tonight, Kerri." He pushes me off his lap. "Go to bed."

"No." I plant my feet. If I have to drag his ass down the hall the man is sleeping in my bed. "We both fucked up. Maybe we should both sleep on the couch."

His eyes darken. "If I come to your bed you won't be sleeping, Numbers." He gives his head a little shake. "Not after the night we've had."

"Maybe that's why I want you there." I'm a little ashamed at the breathy way it comes out of my mouth. I meant to sound confident and sure but instead I sound needy and desperate.

Probably because I am. I'm desperate to have him hold me. I need to believe he can make everything okay.

I need to know we're okay.

He's silent for a minute and I hold my breath, certain he's going to send me off on my own and I'll be alone. Without him.

Evan stands and scoops me up in one smooth move, pulling my legs around his waist as he walks toward my bedroom. We go down to the mattress together, a jumble of limbs, fighting to yank clothes off each other and ourselves. He's inside me before I can take a full breath. No wasting time. No slow-burn. Just his body inside mine.

I hold him tight as he fills me, his lips dragging along my neck.

"I'm so sorry." He murmurs it over and over as he pushes into me, his hips pressing into my thighs with every stroke, dragging me closer to the edge with every glide of his cock, pushing harder and faster until I'm barely hanging on.

His mouth is on mine as one hand moves up to cup the fullness of my breast before rolling the nipple between his fingers. I come undone around him, calling his name as he impales me with one last deep stroke, finding his own release with my name on his lips.

Evan kisses me. My lips, my cheek, my neck. He nuzzles my ear. "You're the only woman I've ever slept with, Kerri."

Between the orgasm and the wine I'm a little groggy so I am quite confident I heard that wrong. "What?"

"I've never slept with another woman. In a bed. All night." He leans up and looks at me. "Only you."

Why does that make me sad?

What if this man has never known real love? Or even real affection?

I'm not sure about the first one yet but the second? I have that. Lots of that one.

I smile up at him. "I guess that makes me special then."

Evan brushes his thumb across my cheek and smiles back.

"You have no idea."

13

Tracker

I ROLL OVER in Kerri's bed and slide my arm across her side expecting to feel the soft warmth of her body beside me.

I don't.

I lean up and look at the pile of cool rumpled blankets where she should be. "Kerri?"

I listen for a second, expecting to hear the sound of her moving through the apartment.

I don't.

I get out of bed. Maybe she's in the bathroom and can't hear me. I reach the doorway. The bathroom door is open and the room is dark.

"Kerr?" The first tickle of concern reaches my belly as I walk into the living room and find it as empty as the rest of the apartment.

Her bag and keys sit on the dining table in the exact spot where they were last night. I walk to the front door and twist the knob, my heart picking up speed with every passing second I don't hear her voice. I pull and the door swings open.

It was unlocked.

I know I locked it last night after everyone left.

The seed of concern in my stomach grows into a gnawing fear as I step out the door into the morning light. Her car's here, parked right next to Hawk's pickup. He sits slack jawed in the seat, his head tipped back against the headrest. I walk to the driver's door in my underwear and bang on the window. He jumps. "What the—" Hawk looks around the parking lot, squinting his eyes against the sun. He looks at me. "What the fuck happened?"

I yank open his door. "Where's Kerri?"

Hawk stares at me for a second. "Kerri?"

"The woman we're here to fucking protect." I point back at Kerri's apartment. "Where is she?"

Hawk's eyes follow my pointing finger and stay there. The color drains from his face. I turn and look, hoping I'll see Kerri standing in the doorway even though I know by the look in his face I won't.

She's not there.

What is there steals the air from my lungs.

Got her

That same messy scrawl in red. My heart stops. I run to the door with Hawk's heavy boots pounding the pavement right behind me. My bare feet skid to a stop at the stoop. I drop down and look for something, anything that might tell me what happened.

A small spray of blood dots the cement just in front of the threshold.

I stand up and turn in a circle, raking my fingers through my hair. "Fuck."

This can't be happening. I was supposed to protect her. I promised her.

She trusted me.

"Get over here now." Hawk's on the phone. His eyes shift to me. He turns away but I still hear what he says. "She's gone."

She's gone.

They have her and God only know what they're doing with her.

I push it out of my mind as I jump over the blood spattered stoop and run into the apartment. I'm dressed and grabbing Kerri's keys off the table when Butch walks up to her front door. He drops down to a squat and looks at the stoop. He brushes a finger over one of the larger spots of blood. It doesn't smear. He lifts his eyes to me. "Any idea when this happened?"

I shake my head once. "The bed was cold when I woke up."

I don't want to consider how long she's been gone. How in the hell I didn't hear whatever happened here. What she was doing. What she was wearing.

Please God let her have put clothes on.

"We have to find her." I step out the door and shut and lock it behind me. I unlock her car with the fob. "Who's in charge of what's going on with The Horsemen?" I look at Hawk, hoping he knows something.

Hawk shrugs. "King's been pretty close mouthed about it."

That means he's got the younger men on it. The ones he knows are behind him. That's probably how we got here in the first place. A bunch of young kids with a chip on their shoulder and something to prove being led by an angry old man.

With a bigger chip on his shoulder and more to prove.

"What about Gypsy? Do we know where he stands?" Gypsy used to be in charge of keeping track of the rival gangs in the area before King moved him to the warehouse, one of the three legitimate businesses the club runs.

Wait.

I look at Butch. "Who else has King moved recently?"

Hawk looks at Butch and then at me. "You think he's trying to push the older members away from the club?"

Butch shakes his head. "He's moving the men he doesn't trust while he pulls the rest close."

"Those are the men who are with us." I pull out my phone and dial Gypsy's number.

"Tracker man. Long time no see."

"Hey. I wish I had time to explain more but I need your help." I hold my breath. If Gypsy refuses I know he's with King and my best shot at finding Kerri before anything happens to her is gone. If he agrees, he could still be with King, but it's a risk well worth taking.

"Sure dude." I hear him yell at someone that he's leaving. "What can I do for you?"

"I need to know where The Horsemen would take someone."

The other end of the line goes silent.

Fuck. I bet wrong.

Finally his voice comes across the line, low and careful. "Anything I could give you will be six months old."

"I know that. I'll take anything you can give me."

"Who've they got?"

I look across the quiet parking lot as the question rolls around in my head. Who is Kerri? She's King's daughter which is what led me here, but now Kerri is more than that.

She's mine.

"My girl. They took her this morning." I glance up at Butch expecting to see at least a little surprise in his eyes. There's none.

"She's King's daughter." I add it in because even though it makes me sick to have to tie her to him, it matters. Being his daughter will mean more to The Horsemen than what she is to me.

"Fuck, dude. Does King know?"

"I sure as hell hope not." It's a weakness he would exploit and it would work.

"You want me to come help you find her?" Gypsy sounds sincere. Has the whole time. I want to agree without taking a breath but that would be stupid and I can't afford to be stupid.

I look to Butch. He nods.

"We do."

For the first time Gypsy sounds leery. "Who's we?"

"Me, Butch, and Hawk." I'm not breathing. I need his help and it's so close.

"Cool. I'll send you an address to meet at. Get there quick though. Those Horsemen dudes are fucking crazy." Gypsy hangs up.

"Who else?" I look at Hawk and Butch. We need more men to cover as much space as we can. "No bikes either. We need to be under the radar."

Butch and Hawk nod.

Hawk pulls his phone out. "I know of three that will help us." He thumbs the screen and taps it before putting it up to his ear.

Butch looks at me as Hawk makes calls. "If we're wrong this whole thing could blow up." He pulls his own phone from his pocket. "All of it. Not just with The Horsemen. The whole club could implode."

"I think there's a good chance that will happen anyway."

The three of us stare at each other for a second.

We're fucked and we're wasting time. We don't have many options and the ones we have are shit.

"If we don't tell King then we're going behind his back and making club decisions on our own. If we do tell him he will fuck it up." I look at Butch and then Hawk. "Are you comfortable doing this? If you want out, tell me now."

I will go find her myself and God help whoever has her. Kerri's the first woman to accept me as more than a piece-of-shit criminal with no family and an ugly past. It's the first time in my life I've ever felt like I was enough.

I'm not losing that for anything. Kerosene Danger Wallace is mine. The first real thing I've ever had.

No one is taking her from me.

I will do whatever it takes to bring her home safe. Fight. Maim.

Murder.

"I'm with you, brother." Butch pats me on the shoulder and looks me straight in the eye. "We'll find her."

I turn my attention to Hawk who's looking up at the sky. He blows out a breath. "We're going to lose everything."

"Does that mean you're out?" I wouldn't hold it against him if it did. I'm the only one who loses if they don't go. I'm the one King will blame for Kerri's kidnapping. I'm the one who will lose Kerri.

Everyone else is better off to lay low and let me take the fall.

He shakes his head. "We have to save her." Hawk looks at me. "She's sort of growing on me."

I pull him in for a slap on the back before I start walking to Kerri's car. "She does that."

****

Gypsy's shaggy blonde hair is longer than the last time I saw him which goes to show how careful King has been about keeping the men he suspects could take him down apart. The same goes for the rest of the ten men assembled in the parking lot of a fast food joint on the east side of Knight territory. But there's no time for catching up, not now.

Not until we find Kerri.

Gypsy lays down an old-school map on the hood of Kerri's car. "This area here is what I think The Horsemen lost to King most recently." His finger traces a narrow band just beyond where we stand now.

"That's what they're pissed about?" It can't be more than a quarter mile total of loss. Is it simply insult added to injury? The straw that broke the camel's back?

King pushed them too many times and now they're pushing him back.

"Nah. They don't care about that." Gypsy looks up at the man to my left. "Tell em what you know."

Wind looks around the group with a skeptical eye.

Gypsy looks at me.

I turn to the man who kept his ear to the ground for the club, listening to the words running between clubs, among dealers, and on the streets. I look Wind in the eye. "I want King out."

I haven't said it until now. Not even to Butch. But I'll lay every fucking card I have on the table to save Kerri. I'd like to think she'd consider doing it for me. Even if she wouldn't, I'd do it for her a million times to get to sleep in her bed again. To smell the spring that surrounds her and feel like I was finally good enough for the fresh start it promises.

Wind doesn't even flinch at my admission. "So you want his spot?"

"No. I just don't want him doing to anyone else what he did to us." I look around the group. "Anyone else think what he does is fucked up?"

Every eye around me shifts because this is what we've become under King's rule. Suspicious. Untrusting of the men we used to think of as brothers.

Hopefully still can.

Gypsy's hand shoots up.

Then Butch and Hawk.

Crow and Preacher follow suit.

Drifter and Cook glance at each other and then turn to me and nod.

Moon raises his pointer finger in the air.

All eyes move to Wind.

He stands tall, arms crossed over his chest as he stares at me, his gaze hard. "The other clubs know King's slipping. They know we're weak."

I shake my head. "We're not weak."

Gypsy nods his head. "They're about to find that out the hard way." He scans the group then drops his finger to the map. "This is their main house. I don't think she's there."

The circle tightens around Gypsy as he lists off the places he thinks The Horsemen might take Kerri and assigns them to two-man groups. When they're all doled out I look around the group of men ready to help me in spite of the risk it poses.

"I owe all of you." I make eye contact with each of my brothers. "Whatever you need, I'll be there."

Gypsy grins at me, bobbing his head in agreement. "Let's go get your girl then."

We split up and fan out to our cars. I jump in the driver's side of Kerri's car as Butch gets in the passenger and we pull out of the lot. It's been almost two hours since I woke up without her.

A fucking long two hours.

But now time is speeding up as I race through town, watching my back to make sure we're not being tailed. The Horsemen know we'll come after her and will most certainly be anticipating our arrival. I glance at Butch. "Have you seen anything?"

He's frowning. "Nothing. Not a damn thing." He glances in his side mirror. "Something's wrong."

I don't have the chance to ask what before my phone rings. My heart picks up. Someone must have found her.

I look at the screen to see who I owe my hind teeth to.

"It's King." I say it out loud because I can't believe it. "Of all the fucking times."

Actually it makes sense in a way that means I'm fucked. We're all fucked.

"Someone's a rat." Butch looks at the ringing phone. "You gotta answer him."

He's right. I connect the call. "Yeah."

"I need you to come to the clubhouse." King doesn't correct my yeah. He definitely knows something's up.

I make the last turn before our assigned location and concentrate on keeping my voice calm and even. "I'd be happy to. How's three?"

"Now." The answer's short and abrupt.

Oh yeah. He knows.

"I'm on my way." I look at Butch before I add the next part. "I'll be there in ten minutes."

"Fine." He hangs up without asking why I'm so close when I'm supposed to be protecting his daughter an hour away.

"He knows they have her." I set the phone in the console as I pull up in front of a boarded up shell of a building with a condemned sign taped to what's left of the smoke singed front door.

"At least we know she's not in there." Butch pulls his phone out of his pocket and sends a message to the rest of the group as I turn around and race down the street.

"Who do you think the mole is?" I think back on the faces of the men who dropped everything to help me. It burns to think that one of them would betray me like this. And not just me.

Nine of us. He betrayed nine of his brothers for a piece of shit man who lures boys into a club with promises of camaraderie and belonging.

Hot food and a place to sleep. King delivers on what he offers.

But asks so much in return.

I speed along the road to the clubhouse, the rage building inside me, riding on the back of the adrenaline pumping through my veins. It's time for King to face the piper. It's his fault The Horsemen have Kerri.

It's his fault she's scared and alone.

And I'm going to remedy that.

I meant it when I said no one was going to stand in my way. I will find Kerri and she will be coming home with me today. Everyone who put her where she is will pay for their part.

Including her daddy.

14

Kerri

NO GOOD FUCKING deed goes unpunished that's for sure.

I stretch my legs out in front of me again and shift on my butt, trying to get the circulation going in the lower half of my body. I wiggle my toes in the slippers I shoved on my feet before going out to check on Hawk.

I kinda thought he was dead this morning. How fucked up is it that my first thought after that was I'm really glad I didn't give that stuff to Evan? It just goes to show no matter how hard I ran from my past I can't escape what I am. What parentage determined I would be.

Half ruthless.

Maybe I deserve to be here just for that.

It's only half though. I didn't *want* Hawk to be dead. Not at all. He's funny as hell once he loosens up.

I'd just rather him be dead than Evan.

Unfortunately based on my current situation I'm the one most likely to end up dead by the end of the day.

And doesn't that fucking suck balls.

I twist at the zip ties around my feet. They cut a little more into the bare skin of my ankles as I try to pull my legs apart and break the lock. It's fucking plastic. How is fucking plastic so damn strong?

I lean back against the wall and scan the room again, starting in the corner by the door. There has to be something here I can use. I need to get these ties off and be ready to do some damage. That means I have to find anything I can use to defend myself when those motherfuckers come back.

And I don't doubt for a minute they'll be back.

The room they locked me in looks like it could be a bedroom, but not a normal kind of bedroom. The walls aren't all drywall. The one containing the only window is cement which makes me think I'm not in a regular sort of house. Not a good thing. Even if I get out of here my chances for finding help go down exponentially if I'm not in a neighborhood with nosy neighbors to run to.

I sink lower as I come up empty for the millionth time. I'm the only thing in the room besides the sheet covering the single cement-wall window. Maybe I could hurl myself out if it came down to it. I'd rather take my chances with a second story window than the pricks who grabbed me the minute I stepped out the door this morning.

At least I got a good swing in on the skinny one before the giant fucker grabbed me and pulled a cover over my head. I tip my head back against the wall and smile at the memory of his nose crunching under the heel of my hand. Score one for self-defense class. The smile is short lived though. Because no matter how many hits I got in the end result is still the same.

I'm here and Evan's going to blame himself.

That's why I have to figure out how to get out of here alive. Because I know what will happen if my father finds out I'm gone.

He'll blame Evan too.

And he'll hurt him worse than these guys plan on hurting me.

A fresh round of tears burns my eyes. I blink them back so hard it hurts. I don't have any more time to waste being scared. For me or for Evan. I have to dig down and be the one thing I never wanted to admit I could be.

Like my father.

I have to find that well of crazy I know lives deep inside me. That shred of his DNA I'm only willing to admit I have because it is what will save me from this predicament. I close my eyes and breathe deep, letting that tiny bit of vicious anger I know I possess grow and unfurl. It burns my belly and heats my skin.

I can do this.

I open my eyes and start over, looking at the room with a fresh perspective. The only part of the space I can't see is the inside of the closet across from me. I stare at it. I have to get in there.

If only they hadn't tied my hands behind my back. I could break the ties if they were in front of me. All I'd have to do is pull them tight and bring my wrists down hard against my body. I've practiced it before. It's not hard. But can I do it the same way from behind?

I'm going to find out. I slide the tie around my wrists until I can reach the free end with my fingers. I pull it as tight as I can and work the lock until it's lined up with the spot where my wrists press together. Now I've just got to get on my feet.

I sit up straight against the wall and tuck my heels as close to my butt as I can get them, pushing up and into the wall at my back, shimmying my way up until I'm on my feet. Barely.

I have to keep my balance because I can't catch myself if I fall and I'll hit the ground hard enough to let whoever is around know that I'm up to something. I take a deep breath as I pull my arms as far back as I can and then bring them down hard against my body.

Nothing.

"Fuck." I keep the word under my breath but it makes me feel better to say it. I fumble around and pull the tie tighter, managing to cinch it a few more clicks, tight enough to cut off the circulation to my hands. I hurry to line the lock up again before I lose the feeling in my fingers.

I pull back again and close my eyes, imagining the face of the man that hits my mom. The man that told me I was a waste of a pussy. The man that will hurt Evan if I fail.

I bring my arms down as hard as I can.

Snap.

The relief is instant. Mentally and physically. I rub my wrists then shake my hands, trying to speed the blood back into my fingers because that tie was only half of my immediate problem.

And that's only the first problem on a long list.

I'm fucked.

It's so hard to fight the feeling of hopelessness that wants to creep in and make me sit back on the floor and cry and wait for Tracker to find me. Again.

I know he's coming. I know he's doing everything to find me.

But what if he can't?

That's why I can't lose my grip on the anger I know can carry me through this. I have to remember the look on my dad's face every time he raised a hand to my mother and me.

He liked it.

And he'll like hurting Tracker too. That's how he gets off. Control.

Proving he's stronger. Meaner. Crazier.

And right now I have to be like him.

I dig my fingernail into the locking mechanism of the thick zip tie around my ankles and shove it down. The tail slides free easily without the tab to click between the grooves.

And now I'm free.

Sort of.

I stand up and walk to the closet with soft steps then gently ease the bi-fold doors open, saying a prayer there's something in there I can use.

Jackpot.

I snag the only item in the closet just as the sound of voices in the hall drift under the door. I grip my weapon with shaky fingers. I've got one chance at this so I have to make it count. I can do this.

Unless there's more than two of them.

Then I'm back to being fucked.

I move to tuck against the line of wall behind the door and force myself to breathe slow. In...

Out...

In...

The lock on the door clicks open. I watch as the knob twists.

Out...

"Hey, Princess. It's showtime." It's the giant of a man. I remember his voice in my ear from the ride here when he detailed all the terrible things his president was going to let them do to me.

In...

The door opens. Skinny is with the giant. There's only two of them and they don't notice me. Their eyes are on the zip ties laying in the middle of the floor.

I kick the door shut and swing my arm as hard and as fast as I can, catching the bigger guy in the temple with the helmet from the closet. He drops like a fly. Number two gapes at me. I swing again, knowing I only have a second before he does more than gape. The helmet cracks against his skull with a sickeningly satisfying thud. He staggers toward me, his eyes bulging.

Oh shit. He didn't go down as easy as the first guy, but he does finally go down, crashing into the wall and sliding down face first. I take a few steps back and watch the two crumpled bodies for any sign of consciousness. They are both out cold.

Holy shit. I didn't really think that would work.

I look down at the helmet in my hand. It served me well but I need something better if I'm going to venture outside this room and that's the next step in my straw house of a plan. I walk over to the big guy and roll him over to his stomach.

The Gods of escape smile down on me for the second time. I slip the pistol out of his waistband and move to his skinny friend. No gun. I pull up his pants leg and my smile from earlier is back. I take off his boot knife sheath and wrap it around my ankle then stand up and suck in another slow breath as I walk to the door. I turn and look at them before I leave. I lean over the big man to whisper in his ear.

"I don't like being called Princess."

Then I see something that makes my blood run cold. Sticking out of the neckline of his shirt is a familiar looking emblem. I grab the collar and yank it down.

No.

I twist and reach for Skinny grabbing the neckline of his shirt. I pull it down and my blood goes from cold to ice.

They're Knights.

The rage I worried wouldn't appear burns like fire through my body as I stand up and stare at the door.

I was wrong. I can never be like my father.

I will be worse.

I tip my head from side to side, stretching out the tension from hours on the fucking floor. The floor of The Knights' clubhouse.

Because it was my father who had me kidnapped.

And now it's time for him to be punished. I've done what it took to protect myself from King and I'm not fucking stopping now.

I press my ear to the door. The hall is quiet outside. I crack it open and peer out. Now I can hear voices coming from downstairs. I slide into the dimly lit corridor and toe my way across the plywood covering the floor, catching one foot on a fire extinguisher as I go. I barely manage to grab it before it topples over. I slide it close to the wall and continue on. The voices get louder and I can see the space opens up into a vaulted ceiling ahead.

"You are going to pay for what you've done to me."

It's my piece of shit father and he can only be talking to one person.

I press into the wall and ease toward the edge, crouching behind the banister to peek over the open great room where three men stand with their backs to me...

And two men sit facing the stairs, strapped to chairs with the same zip ties that were used on me.

Those men are the only two I'm worried about.

The others can fucking rot as far as I'm concerned. One in particular.

I ease back out of sight, pretending I didn't see the blood running from Tracker's beat up face.

I have one gun and one knife and there are three of them, all definitely armed. I can't just start shooting them. Then I'll be dead along with Tracker and Butch. I have to get them to come to me. I look back down the long hallway. It's lined with closed doors. I can't imagine anyone is in the rooms when there's a show to watch going on downstairs. But if there is someone in one I have a plan.

I'll shoot them. That'll bring the guys running upstairs toward me that's for sure.

I'll make that plan B.

I open the first door, careful to be quiet. It's someone's living quarters. The room's immaculate.A perfectly made bed with crisp sheets sits in the center of the room. My eyes zero in on the nightstand. I pad across the floor and slide open the drawer, pushing around the loose condoms and lube until I find what I was hoping for. I grab it and yank as many blankets off the bed as I can before creeping back into the hallway and laying them just below a smoke alarm with a green light glowing on the face. I snap the lighter I found in the drawer and lay it against the linens.

"Burn baby burn."

I'm gonna burn King's whole fucking world to the ground for what he did to me.

The cotton catches immediately. I grab the fire extinguisher sitting on the floor and go back to the bedroom. While the smoke builds I check the tag on the extinguisher. It's ten years old. Probably came with the damn building. It had to be one of the members that brought it here after they stuck the smoke alarm to the ceiling because I can't imagine my father taking the time to make sure this place is up to code. It's not like *he* sleeps here.

Hopefully the thing still works.

The smoke alarm starts to scream. I tuck the pistol in the back of my shorts then pull the pin from the extinguisher handle and wait.

"What the fuck?" I hear my father's roar over the sound of a couple more alarms that join the first as the smoke spreads down the hall.

Boots race up the stairs toward me. I can't tell how many.

The first man rushes past the door without looking in with the second man from downstairs close on his heels. This one looks in the open door. I can't wait any longer to see if my father is with them. I have to act now.

I squeeze the handle and spray number two square in the face with chemical-filled foam until he slams back into the wall. I step to the doorway and aim at his friend, nailing him before he can warn anyone. Now they can barely sputter, let alone scream a warning to their president.

And I'm coming for him next.

I set down the extinguisher and walk toward the stairs, pulling the pistol from my waistband

and switching off the safety. Bet King's going to regret trying to make me like him before he realized what a pain in the ass I was and started smacking me instead of teaching me how to run in his world.

It looks like I learned enough to get by.

He's running up the stairs yelling for the two men struggling to breathe in the hall as I reach the landing, my pistol aimed between his eyes. He stops at the second-to-last step.

"Hey there." I'm proud of how cold I sound. "How's your day going?" I step toward him and begin descending the stairs. For every step I take forward, he takes one backward. "Funny seeing you here." I tip my head to one side. "What with me supposedly being kidnapped by some rival gang."

"Put the gun down, bitch." He takes a step back.

"You don't tell me what to do anymore. Remember?" I step forward.

He sneers at me. "That was always your problem. Didn't know your place."

246

"Is that what this is about?" I step toward him. "Teaching me my place?"

"Stupid cunt. Nothing's ever been about you."

My finger twitches.

"Don't do it, Kerri." I hear Evan's voice over the ear piercing ring of the alarms screaming as the smoke spreads, creeping into the air around me.

I relax my finger just a little and blink against the burning in my eyes.

My father's face twists into a sick sort of smile. "Lookie there. Maybe you can be taught after all."

And then he lunges at me.

I don't hear the shot but I know it happened. I felt it.

I wish I could say it didn't feel a little good.

King's eyes go wide as the blood starts to trickle down his shoulder.

Maybe I didn't want to kill him as much as I thought I did.

I point the gun between his eyes again. "Turn around and start walking." I tilt the gun sideways because I mean business and I figure that might be a good way to convey the sentiment. "Unless you want to die in here which I'm okay with too."

My father's nostrils flare as he turns. I grab his piece from the back of his pants and tuck it into mine as we walk. The zip ties they used to secure Tracker and Butch to the chairs they sit in still lay on the table in the living area. I keep my gun pointed as I flip Skinny's knife out of its sheath and cut Evan free. I nod to the ties then look at my father with a smirk. "Tie him up."

Guess who calls the shots now motherfucker?

Tracker grabs the ties as I cut Butch free.

I point to the stairs as Butch stands up. "There's four guys upstairs. Two unconscious and two in the hallway. Let's try to get them out of here before it's too late." Butch nods and takes off.

Tracker double ties King and pushes him my way. "Take this outside while I help Butch." He gives me a wink with his less swollen eye. This might be the best gift a man has ever given me. Getting to drag my father from the life he created with fear and manipulation.

I smile sweetly at the man who has taken so much from me. Today I got to take everything from him. His club. His freedom. His power.

I grab King by the arm I shot and drag him to the door, liking the wince of pain across his face.

"Betcha didn't see this coming did you?"

Honestly, neither did I.

15

Tracker

SHE BURNED DOWN the fucking clubhouse.

I pull Kerri in tighter to my side and press a painful kiss against the top of her head. I wince as I pull away and wait for the sting to ease before I do it again.

It's worth the pain.

"What happens now?" Kerri looks away from the burnt out pile of rubble left after the fire department finally managed to get the blaze under control.

"I don't know." I look at Butch. "Any ideas?"

to the hospital. She went to the police station to give a statement, so I did too. After almost losing her today she'll be lucky if I let her pee alone. "Just remember your mom has never been on her own before. She's going to have no clue what to do."

"I think she'll be okay." Kerri rests her head against my chest. "I bet she's stronger than she knows."

I chuckle. "You have to get it from somewhere."

Her head tips back and she looks at me. "Is that really where you think it comes from?"

I see the tears edging her eyes and it breaks my heart. "You aren't like him. Not even a little bit."

"But what I did—"

"What you did was fight your own fight and everyone else's. You were brave and strong and did what had to be done." I shook my head at her. "King would never do any of that. He is a coward who preys on broken boys. Pulling them in and using them for his own gain."

Her chin quivers. "But now they don't have a place to live because of me."

I brush my thumb across her bottom lip. "You saved them from your father. Even if they don't think so now, you did them a favor."

She looks at the line of men gathered in the industrial lot. "What about you guys? My dad employed all of you right? What happens to you?"

"I won't be surprised if we discover a certain Jill Wallace is the proud owner of more businesses than she knows what to do with." I looked at my brothers then back at her. "Including the ones these men work at."

Once again I'm happy King was out for himself. Moving all of us away from the inner workings of the club worked out in our favor in the long run.

Kerri lifts her brows and stares at the ground. I can see her mind working behind her dark eyes. "We need an attorney."

I turn from the building. I'm tired of staring at it. "Tomorrow we will work on all of this." I ease Kerri toward the car. "Tonight we're going to check on your mother and then we're going home."

She sniffs. I get her situated in the passenger seat of her car and shut the door before turning to my friends. "I can't thank you guys enough for what you did today."

Gypsy wrinkles his brow at me. "We didn't get to do shit." He nods to the car where Kerri sits. "I'm gonna need to hear the full story of what happened here sometime."

I point to him. "Actually we need you to help get the full story on what happened here today. What's been happening while we were all shuffled around." I step in closer. "I don't think this is over. I don't think King's Knights are going to just lie down and take what happened."

The way the men around me look, they don't think it's over either.

Butch looks my way. "I think King will use whoever is left on his side to come back at us if he can. He might take some time to reorganize but I don't think he will go down this easy."

I glance back at the car and the woman in the front seat. I promised to protect her from him.

I failed.

I won't fail her again.

I nod at Butch. "I'll work on getting King's wife set up with a lawyer and find out where we stand on the businesses and properties." I look around the group. "See what you guys can find out about who he has left that could cause problems." I look at Gypsy. "Find out if there was ever any issue with The Horsemen."

He squints at me in the low evening sun as it stretches across the lot. "You think he made it all up?"

I blow out a breath. This has been the most fucked up day of my life. And I've had a fucked up life. "I don't know what I think. I just know I wouldn't put anything past him."

Butch glances toward the car. "Go get her home." He lifts his arm to pat me on the shoulder but winces, bracing it with his hand as he lowers it. "Take care of her."

I start to walk away but Butch catches me with a hand on my chest. "Make sure she knows we owe her."

I shake my head. "You don't want that." I manage a lopsided grin with the less swollen side of my mouth. "That woman is vicious."

And I fuckin' love it.

Epilogue

Kerri

I WATCH FROM my spot tucked in the corner of the smoky bar. The reason I'm here sits in a corner booth surrounded by friends. His face is serious. Too serious.

Maybe I can do something about that when the time's right.

I sip at my drink, waiting.

I'll wait all night if that's what it takes. I can be patient.

Finally he gets up and slips through the crowd toward the back hall. I slide out of my seat and weave my way after him, dodging dancing couples and waitresses carrying trays of liquor to the outlying tables.

The sound in the main bar is overpowering. Loud conversations and thumping bass fog the air with noise. But the hall is oddly quiet. Just like the first night I met him.

The night I did what it took to escape him. What I thought he represented.

And look at me now. Hunting him the way he tried to hunt me.

Only I'm good at it.

I smile at the jab. I'll have to remember to point out who has the better tracking skills in our relationship. Maybe we could switch names. I'll be Tracker and he can be Numbers.

Fitting since I hear he has the highest grade in his math class at the college.

Suddenly I'm caught from behind and shoved roughly into the men's room by a tall hard body.

"Damn it." I spin around. "How did you see me?"

Evan pushes up against my body, pressing me against the wall as his hands slide up my sides. "I don't need to see you to know you're there." He tips his head and bites my neck as one hand skates across my breast. "I can feel you."

I roll my eyes. "It was the dress wasn't it."

He leans back, his eyes dark. "You don't wear a red dress when you're tailing someone Numbers." His gaze rakes down my front. "Especially this red dress and this someone." He dips his finger under the neckline and tugs it down exposing my breast to the heat of his stare. "I do love this fucking dress though." Evan leans down to suck my nipple between his teeth growling against my skin as I gasp.

"I might love you." My head tips back as he snags the other side of my dress and bares my other breast.

His mouth hovers over my untouched nipple making it tighten in anticipation. "Might?"

I grab at the back of his head and try to arch into him, needing to feel the pull of his mouth.

"Why do you do this to me?" I squirm around, trying to get the contact I want from him.

He manages to elude every attempt I make. "Because you like it." Evan lifts the hem of my skirt, dragging the stretchy fabric up my thighs. "You like when I make you wait."

"That's not true." I shake my head as the cool air of the bathroom hits the uncovered skin of my pussy. "I like it when you give me what I want immediately."

He lifts an eyebrow at me. "Do you?" He grabs my naked ass with both hands and groans. "Jesus, Kerri. No panties?"

"I wanted you to know I'm a sure thing." My breath catches as he uses his grip on my ass to lift me off the ground. "Besides you're notoriously difficult to get in the sack." I smile against Tracker's neck as he scoffs.

"That was one time." He pushes my upper body tighter against the wall. "And you were trying to use me."

"Who says I'm not now?"

Evan leans back and grins at me. "Maybe now I like it."

I moan softly as he pushes inside me. The door to the bathroom starts to open and he kicks his leg back, slamming it shut.

"Occupied." His voice is low and rough as he snaps at whatever poor unsuspecting man tried to interrupt us.

I start to smile but he's suddenly fucking me deep and fast, redirecting my focus in an instant. "God you are so good at this."

"I aim to please." He grinds against me with every thrust, rubbing my clit with each stroke. His lips find my nipple, sucking it deep into the liquid heat of his mouth and I come, clenching around his cock as Evan buries himself deep inside me with one final push.

"Kerri." His breathing is raspy in my ear, as we come together. He sags against me for a few seconds, catching his breath. Once his ragged breathing evens out Evan drops a few kisses down the line of my jaw. "I love you."

I pull him tight against me. "I love you too."

He drops my feet to the floor, waiting until my wobbly legs are steady in my stilettos before easing my skirt back into place and wrapping the spent condom in a paper towel, shoving the wad through the louvered trash can lid. He pulls me against him for another kiss.

I slide my hands along his neck, gliding over the spot that used to mark him as a Knight. Now it's covered with a brightly colored flower that vines through the dark hues marking his body. He says it signifies the first bright spot in what started as a sad life.

"I have to go finish my meeting with the boys." He kisses my nose. "And they're expecting you to join us."

"What?"

Evan laughs loudly as he opens the bathroom door, holding me tight against his side as we walk into the hallway. He shoots the wide-eyed man waiting outside a nod and leans down to my ear. "If you think I'm the only guy in this bar who noticed the hot blonde drinking alone in the corner then you're crazy."

I look up at the man who is everything I thought I never wanted and smile.

"I thought that was why you liked me?"

"That's not the only reason, Numbers." He squeezes my ass as we reenter the bar.

"Not by a long shot."